# Bold in America

## A Young Man Steps out into the World and Discovers the Truth About Himself

by

Karen Gustafson

Karen Gustaf

**RED LEAD PRESS**
**PITTSBURGH, PENNSYLVANIA 15222**

The contents of this work including, but not limited to, the accuracy of events, people, and places depicted; opinions expressed; permission to use previously published materials included; and any advice given or actions advocated are solely the responsibility of the author, who assumes all liability for said work and indemnifies the publisher against any claims stemming from publication of the work.



ISBN: 978-1-4349-6257-7
Printed in the United States of America

*First Printing*

For more information or to order additional books, please contact:
Red Lead Press
701 Smithfield Street
Pittsburgh, Pennsylvania 15222
U.S.A.
1-800-834-1803
*www.redleadbooks.com*

This novel is in honor or Jesus Christ who is leading me on a wonderful life adventure, and to my parents who are selflessly loving and supporting me as the adventure unfolds.

# Foreword

"Fitting in" is so important to many of us, and, often, the more we strain after it, the more elusive it becomes. In this novel Bold really does want to be part of the world around him, and he thinks that he is, when he is at home in Zuunmod, Mongolia. But stepping out into the world, Bold leaves behind the insulated world in which he has grown up and is forced to examine the person he is and face the question of who it is he wants to become. The deep loneliness he experiences, and the emptiness he discovers inside first makes him angry and then leads him to ask questions of what life is supposed to be all about. I hope that you enjoy this story as you think about your own adventure into life.

# Chapter 1:
# The Opportunity

Saraa slammed her books down on the table next to Bold. She had arrived late to first hour. Ortonjargal Bagsh had berated her, and Bold knew better than to say even a word of greeting. He waited quietly, keeping his eyes on the teacher, but his ears and heart tuned towards Saraa. She furiously wrote on a corner of her notebook page, "He did it again!"

That was all she had to write. Rage tightened Bold's jaw and reddened his throat and cheeks. Besides the fact that they were in math class, Bold's sense that Saraa had already begun to calm down and to engage in class allowed him to maintain some control. Saraa's stepfather routinely drank too much and then kept her up half the night, banging on her bedroom door, which, fortunately, had a lock on the inside. Her mother worked nights at the sewing factory, so she could not stop her husband. Saraa had to protect herself and her younger sisters.

"Saraa, why don't you move out? You could live with Baaggii, your older sister." Bold had asked when he first learned of Saraa's home situation.

Saraa refused, "I can't just leave my younger sisters; they wouldn't stand a chance against him. He's disgusting. And even though he's a klutz when he's drunk, he's still bigger than they are and quite strong." She chose to stay and fight, even if it meant not sleeping some nights and arriving at school late.

Bold's rage at Saraa's stepfather vied with his admiring love for Saraa as he covertly glanced at her. Despite the fact that her dark brown uniform was worn and getting too short, Bold thought it suited her. Saraa's deep brown eyes, previously sparking with fury now danced with intellectual interest at the lesson. Her full lips slightly parted and pursed themselves as if she was drinking in the formulas on the board. Her sleek black hair swung across her back as she wrote quickly to catch up with the notes for the day. She glanced his way and smiled, sending electricity through his veins.

Bold sighed and returned his focus to math, a subject that seemed to suit Saraa much better than it suited him. Physical education was his favorite, even when they just did conditioning. Then his 6-foot frame could stretch and not feel so confined as it often did in the classroom. Even English class, his best subject if someone looked at his grades, made him feel confined. The fact that his mother was the teacher helped his grades, but intensified his impatience with the clock that ticked off the time.

Throughout the day Bold listened as Saraa recounted her night of battle. "Then he fell backwards over the coffee table, landing in the chair. He got comfortable and forgot his mission for a couple of hours, giving us a break. Oyuna and Naraa fell asleep at that point." Saraa grinned at the memory, drawing a matching grin from Bold. "As long as I have you to talk to, it'll be okay," she assured him.

They exited the school for the day, holding hands, an act of open affection that would not have been tried in Zuunmod a decade earlier. Bold's father had been telling him about the "old days" the night before, reminding Bold to be ever thankful that Mongolia was finally entering the 21st Century.

The lecture had been precipitated by the upcoming visit from Bold's English coach, Todd. Bold's mother had insisted that Bold invite Todd for dinner to thank him for working with the students on English in an after-school club. She made sure Bold attended every Tuesday and Thursday, even if Bold thought he had something more important to do. At first Bold had resented going and had sat on the edge of the group, refusing to participate. Just because his mother was the best English teacher in the town and his father was the chief of police did not mean he had to constantly perform to keep the family's reputation intact, did it?

Well, it actually did. "Reputation is everything in Zuunmod. You know it's the central aimag of Mongolia, and, therefore, people expect great things from its people. This is where leaders can be born," Bold's grandfather had told him last summer as they sat on the hillside watching the herd. "One day you'll cash in on your parents' good names, and so you must honor what they are doing now for you and your sisters. Life is tough enough without trying to make it alone. People help those who can one day help them, so that making a good name through hard work and honor is key to your future."

"Well, I guess I'd better get to my sister's. She leaves for work soon. I'll see you after basketball, right?" Saraa startled Bold back into the present. Their silent walk had taken them to the end of the street near her sister's building. Embarrassed to have been so distracted, Bold smiled into her eyes and quickly pecked her waiting lips.

"Right. I can't wait. See if you can get the little ugly one down for a nap before I get there." Bold accepted her playful punch on the arm, knowing that she understood he adored the "ugly one" and would romp with her on the floor while Saraa did her homework.

Playing basketball released Bold like nothing else ever did. Even time spent with Saraa kept him on edge and concerned with what he said and how he said it. He preferred games like today when few words were spoken, and the panting and grunting of his friends expressed it all. Before he had had enough, Bold tore himself away. He had to get to Saraa early today, so he could be home in time to help his father with the dinner. Afterall, it was supposedly for him that they were having Todd over. Bold shrugged off the thought as he tugged on his sweatshirt. Todd wasn't so bad. It would be a good night. Company always put his parents into a good mood, at least while the company was there.

"Hi, Todd, come on in. I'll get you some tea." Bold greeted his English coach who seemed to tower over him at 6'5". It always amazed Bold to feel short around someone when he tended to be the one looking down on others. It had been part of what drew Bold into the discussions and had helped him decide to find out what made this Peace Corp volunteer decide to come to an unimportant country like Mongolia.

"Thanks, Bold. This is so nice of you all. I hope it hasn't made a lot of extra work for your mom. I know that she works hard as it is." Todd impressed Bold with his knowledge of Mongolian custom, as well as his ability to speak Mongolian.

"Actually, my dad is cooking. He makes the best Chinese food you'll ever eat," Bold grinned, using a phrase they had just learned in English club that week. "You may speak English, Todd; it's good practice for me and mom. I've been told I'll be translator for the evening, though, so don't speak too quickly."

"Sounds like a plan," Todd grinned back as he accepted the cup of milk tea offered him. "Thanks." Silence ensued as Todd sipped the tea and Bold busied himself setting out dishes.

The meal passed all too quickly with only spurts of conversation as new dishes were constantly brought out, and Todd complimented everything he ate. Bold's parents finally joined them and filled their own rice bowls with a variety of meats and vegetables. Bold preferred the meat dishes, as any Mongolian would, but his dad could make even vegetables taste good, so he tried everything. He did not eat as much as he usually would because nerves took up space in his stomach. After the meal they would sit around and talk, testing Bold's ability to really speak and understand English. Since his mother was his English teacher, she'd know if he tried to bluff his way through this. He knew she wouldn't tell his father, but he'd still feel shame.

"That was fantastic. Thank you," Todd patted his flat stomach as he sat back on the couch. "You are an incredible cook, Erdene." Bold translated, seeing pleasure light up his father's eyes.

"How do you like Mongolia?" Bold translated to Todd.

"I love it," Todd responded enthusiastically.

The niceties were easy to translate. Bold could tell that Todd and his mother were rooting for him and that his father was watching carefully to make sure the conversation made sense. It took a while for Bold to realize that his father was uncomfortable being the only one unable to speak English. This was a kind of shame for his father.

"Todd can speak Mongolian, too," Bold contributed when a lull presented itself.

His father's eyes lit up as he sat forward and asked Todd, in Mongolian, about his family. Todd answered the question, and the conversation continued with only a few errors on Todd's part. Everyone laughed when he asked if the meat used in the first dish had been "huuni maxh" (human meat) instead of "hooni maxh" (mutton). People relaxed, and both languages blended together so that people could connect and truly begin to know each other.

Tension did return, however, when the topic of religion came up. Todd asked about the altar at the end of the living room. Narangerel, Bold's mother, explained her Buddhist beliefs and traditions. Then Todd asked Erdene what he believed.

"Many Mongolians are Buddhist, it is true, but I am an atheist." Bold had trouble translating that word, but his mother unobtrusively slipped it in for him. "I grew up under the Communist education system brought by the Russians. They were very good to us and helped Mongolia move forward." A challenge seemed to fire from his father's eyes.

Todd's clear blue eyes and friendly, open face merely accepted what his father asserted. "I believe in Jesus." He responded.

*Well, of course he does*, Bold thought. *Didn't all Americans?*

"Who is Jesus?" His father asked.

"He is the Son of God, who came and lived as a man. He was perfect and did not do anything evil, so that when He died He became a sacrifice for all the evil you and I have ever done. He makes it possible for us to know the Creator God."

"That is impossible. No human can be perfect. Besides, there is no God. If there was, the world would be a much better place. People would not starve or fight wars. This is why I am an atheist." Erdene's contempt for Todd's beliefs threatened to spoil the evening. His mother quickly changed the subject.

"Todd, Bold brought home this letter about going to America."

Now it was Bold's turn to be surprised. He had not shown his mother the letter, which Todd had given him at English Club. He had tossed it in his book bag, forgetting about it the minute he received it. Sure, America sounded like a wonderful place, but he would never go there. He liked his life here in Zuunmod.

"It's a great opportunity. I think Bold would really learn a lot from it, and not just English. He could experience the culture and see what life is like in a different place. He is my best student in English Club." Todd's enthusiasm drew Bold's parents into the idea.

Bold saw the pride glow on his mother's cheeks and in her eyes. To compliment an English teacher's son on his English was one of the highest compliments one could pay. However, Bold knew the truth. He had learned to pick up just enough of Todd's words to ask questions that kept Todd talking. When it came to questions, if he watched Todd closely enough, he could figure out an appropriate response, whether he really understood the question or not. So, Bold had conquered the art of conversation in English, but he was not sure he could survive in a world that used only that language. Then again, he had done well this evening. It often surprised him to realize how much he did understand during Todd's discussions.

"How does it work? What would we have to do?" Erdene's reserve communicated knowledge of how the world really worked, along with a reminder to Bold that he should be paying attention. He understood his father's meaning, "Nothing is free in this world." Despite the fact that they were one of the more stable families in the community did not mean they had money or connections to make something like this happen.

Bold watched in a daze as his parents discussed his life with Todd. No one even asked him what he wanted. His mind recalled magazine pictures and photographs of America that Todd had brought to class, as well as the mental images he had created with his words. "America must be like heaven," Bold had often thought, but the thought that anyone in their family might ever experience it first hand had been his mother's dream, not his.

"Thanks again. The meal was delicious, and I enjoyed the conversation." Todd shook each person's hand.

"You're welcome. We'll fill out the application, and Bold will return it to you at English Club tomorrow." Narangerel's excitement sparkled in her words, energized her vigorous handshake and shot out of her eyes. This would happen; she would see to that. And she did.

# Chapter 2: Expectations

Bold readjusted his six-foot frame into the window seat of row 38, knowing that soon he'd be sharing the space with two other passengers. He shifted in his seat, there just was not enough space for him, two other passengers and the jumble of emotions that constantly spilled out around him. Eagerness for the adventure to really begin clashed with anxiety over the question of his preparedness.

"Hi, I guess we'll be traveling together. I'm Rhonda." A middle-aged woman smiled as she tossed one small suitcase in the luggage holder above their heads and her oversized purse into the middle seat. Clutching the purse onto her lap she plunged into the seat. Her large frame took up the entire seat, and her long, speckled hair that contained more grey than yellow, threatened to reach over and tickle Bold's nose.

"Hi, my name is Bold." He responded as red embarrassment crept into his sun-browned cheeks. Her nearness did not bother him; after all, riding the van to Ulaan Baatar, the capitol, often meant sharing space with several people packed onto the bench seat, but her flowery scent imposed itself on him, causing him to breathe all the more deeply.

"Is this your first time to America, Bold?"

Her words stuck to each other, making it difficult for Bold to distinguish them. He understood "America" in the midst of unfamiliar sounds and guessed at what she wanted to know. "Yes." His eyes shifted away, covering the dread that the conversation would continue for the next 14 hours of flight.

"Well, if you have any questions, just ask," Rhonda, patted his arm and cast expectant eyes his way.

What had she asked? What was expected of him? He hadn't even left Mongolia, and he already felt certain that he would not be able to function in this new place with its strange language. Thankfully their third seatmate joined them just at that time. Unfortunately, he turned out to be another foreigner, or "gadad huun." The stranger reminded Bold of Todd, except he was not as tall. All outsiders, especially Americans, looked alike to Bold.

"Hey," he tossed off to Rhonda. "Sainbainuu," he greeted Bold, taking more time and looking more intently.

Automatically, Bold responded, "Sain, sainbainuu." Bold's 17-year-old mind and body relaxed as the lanky man of about 20 years old chatted with Bold in his native language.

"My name's Jordan; what's yours?" Jordan's odd accent was another trait that distinguished him from Todd.

"My name is Boldbaatar. But you may call me Bold."

"I recognize the language but don't understand it. Do you two want to sit by each other?" Rhonda barged into their conversation.

"That's okay," Jordan assured her. "I plan on sleeping most of the way. I've about run out of my knowledge of Mongolian anyway." He winked at Bold, translated their exchange with more adeptness than one would expect and then settled into his seat, legs extended, pillow placed behind his neck and eyes closed.

Bold quickly followed suit, realizing this would be the best way for him to survive the long flight to America. He slept a few hours, finally being able to relax after the last week that had been filled with parties with friends, basketball games with his buddies, special dinners with family members, and time with Saraa who had showed a mixture of pride, happiness and sadness at his going. He had not slept at all during the final 48 hours as he packed and said good-bye to the constant assault of visitors. He appreciated the gifts of money they had brought, though, and again felt the thick wad of money that now filled his new wallet.

Bold woke with a start from a dream in which he tried to ask directions to his host-family's house. No one could help him because no one understood his words. He could not even understand what he was trying to say. What was he doing going to America where no one knew Mongolian? How was he ever going to survive? Panic seized Bold's heart and intestines. The need to get up and move propelled him out of his seat, causing him to bump his head on the luggage rack above.

"Excuse me, may I go, please?" He stammered to Rhonda who was reading the airline's magazine.

"Sure, honey," Rhonda jostled the sleeping form next to her, which immediately became alert.

"Hey, do you need to see a man about a horse?" Jordan grinned as he asked Bold in both English and Mongolian.

"Yes, I do," Bold exchanged grins. It helped to hear the familiar request, which sounded so much more polite than the blunt way Americans announced to everyone that they "had to go to the bathroom." Bold gratefully stepped past his seatmates, hoping that the bathrooms would be in the back of the plane, the direction he was headed.

Bold saw a door which appeared to lead to a restroom, but wasn't sure how to tell if anyone was inside. He gently knocked just as another passenger approached from behind.

"You don't have to knock. Just push it open. This sign here says, 'vacant;' that means no one's in there."

Red enflamed Bold's neck and reached up to his cheeks as his eyes traveled to the man's face so that Bold could thank him for his help. The mocking laughter that greeted Bold kidnapped his words and his breath, holding them hostage in his throat. Embarrassment melted into anger. A shove at the door provided escape as the door folded inward. The close confines of the toilet room did nothing to help Bold relax. He gasped for breath and wished that he could slam his fist into something. Instead he took care of business. By the time Bold figured how to flush the toilet, the violent suction also pulled his emotions down the drain. Bold cooled himself off with a splash of water and carefully dried his face and hands.

He felt a moment of panic when he faced the door and had no idea how to get out of it. He stopped breathing again, as he searched for a solution. The memory of pulling the knob to lock it into place flashed behind his eyes, and he gathered together his composure before reentering the plane. His eyes quickly took in his surroundings, hoping the man from earlier would not be there to mock him further. Relief allowed him to breathe again as he made his way back to seat 38A without any scrutiny from fellow passengers.

Bold barely noticed his seatmates as he plopped himself back into the window seat and pulled the blanket of feigned sleep over himself. His father had warned him that he would be getting himself into one predicament after another if he left their hometown. Bold knew that his father, the local chief of police, admired Bold's courage to take on the challenge, but he also had paid the greatest price to help make it happen.

Erdene, Bold's father had called in a lot of favors to collect the $5,000 needed for the trip. He would spend the rest of his life paying off the debt, which did not include only money. People would feel free to demand help with moving, family concerns and even legal matters now. That was the way things worked in his country, and Bold's father had willingly supported his son, but had also realistically admonished Bold that the road ahead would not be easy.

Bold had to make this work. It cost everyone too much for him to blow it. These thoughts bore into his mind as he drifted into sleep. His dreams were haunted by wolves attacking herds of sheep and goats, and of criminals terrorizing Zuunmod as they held his father captive in a cell.

"Excuse me, would you like your meal now?"

Bold started awake to the smell of hot food. His stomach responded with a gurgle and then a growl. Fortunately, his grogginess gave him time to translate the next question.

"Do you want chicken or beef?" The perky stewardess whipped off the choice.

"Beef, please," Bold murmured.

"What would you like to drink?" She asked as she handed him a hot aluminum tray.

"Coke, please," Bold requested, giving the only drink he could think of quickly.

He accepted the drink and observed Rhonda out of the corner of his eye. She bowed her head and prayed over her meal. Whenever Bold had visited Todd at home, Todd had prayed before eating the meals he threw together for himself and Bold. Bold had liked the sense of peace that seemed to settle around them, but had never pursued the topic with Todd.

Bold, himself, didn't care about religion. He supposed there might be a God; after all, someone must be responsible for the making the world, but that God would hardly be concerned with individual lives. The world was too messed up to think that a compassionate God was involved in any of it; he agreed with his dad on this point. People were responsible for making their own lives work. That's exactly what Bold was doing on this plane.

Bold directed his attention once again to figuring out how to eat. Unlike Rhonda, Jordan enthusiastically dug into his meal. Bold mimicked their movements as they ate, carefully lifting the lid off the strange container. Steam singed his knuckles, and revulsion filled his eyes. His stomach churned at the sight of stringy meat smothered in a rusty colored sauce that invaded limp looking vegetables and potato squares.

Hunger compelled Bold to try the food, but the assault of the foreign tastes on his tongue created a revolt in his system. Bold resigned himself to the roll and the coke, reminding himself that he had gone much longer with no food. When his father's cousins from the countryside came to visit, they had to stretch food that normally fed four of them to quell the hunger of 10 people.

Bold casually covered up his uneaten food, pushed aside his aluminum tray and slumped back into his sleep position. This time he immediately fell into a dreamless sleep.

"Hey, Bold, we're here." Rhonda shook his shoulder gently.

Jordan helped Bold through customs, showing him how to fill out the forms. The moment had finally arrived to meet the Bowers. They had sent Bold a picture, so he would know them, but he found that most Americans looked alike to him. Maybe they would recognize him from the picture he had sent.

Passing through the glass doors felt like entering an alien spacecraft for Bold. People clustered around the door with expectant faces, searching for loved ones. No one looked familiar with his or her light hair and pale skin. Even their eyes lacked the rich color Bold had grown up around. He was given little time to process the differences, however, because soon after he exited the customs' area, a little girl with yellow pigtails and light blue eyes catapulted herself into him.

Gasping for air, Bold looked up to see a man, woman and two American boys surround him. "Cammy, let the guy have some space," the tallest boy commanded the over-enthusiastic girl hanging onto Bold's waist. The laughter in the boy's voice told Bold that he was merely being polite and that Cammy probably hugged strangers all the time.

"Hi, I'm Matt Bowers," the man stepped forward with an extended hand. Bold shook the hand, receiving a firm shake but wondering at the smoothness of the palm. His own hand was rough and calloused from working with the herds in the summer and cutting wood all year long.

"Nice to meet you, Mr. Bowers. My name is Bold." Bold grimaced as he felt the familiar red creep into his cheeks.

"Welcome, Bold. I'm Cheryl." The woman immediately inserted herself into the exchange, extending her small, manicured hand.

If Bold had thought Mr. Bowers' hand was smooth, he could not believe the softness of Mrs. Bowers' hand. His mother's hands were often chapped from all of the washing in cold water she did. Such hands must not do any work. Bold wondered if he had been invited to do work for them. Maybe that was what this exchange program was all about. How many students did they have?

"I'm David," the taller boy confidently met Bold's eyes as he shook hands. Was that a challenge Bold saw in his eyes?

"I'm Michael, and this is Cammy," the younger boy grinned and gave a quick shake of the hand as he patted Cammy's back. Cammy shyly proffered her hand and gave a limp shake as Bold's massive hand swallowed hers.

"Let's get your stuff and get home. You must be exhausted." Cheryl Bowers' eyes sparkled with friendliness and concern. Bold realized that despite their pale color they still held many emotions.

"We're glad you're here, Bold," Mr. Bowers clapped him on the shoulder and directed him towards door leading outside.

Cammy slid in next to him and began to pelt him with questions. "Do you like to play hopscotch? What about Chutes and Ladders? Do you know how to skip rope? What do kids play in Mongolia?"

Bold's feeling of being overwhelmed must have been legible in his face which deepened in color. He wondered if he'd ever be able to have a real conversation with these people. They spoke so fast, especially Cammy, who looked up at him as if he were an idiot when he could not respond immediately.

*I'm not an idiot*, he told himself. *I just don't know all these new words they are throwing at me.* Again anger replaced the shame, and he knew the red in his cheeks must have deepened still more. He withdrew into a chilling silence, claiming he was just too tired to talk. The Bowers graciously accepted his appeal and left him alone, but Cammy's confused questions and the brothers' sideways glances told Bold that all was not well. He had blown it, and yet he *almost* didn't care.

The drive from the airport to Remmington, Minnesota, took over three hours. Bold opted for the escape of feigned sleep. At least he had learned something. The Bowers spoke in whispers, trying not to disturb him and assuming that he must be exhausted after his 14-hour plane ride. He was exhausted, but it was from the first hour of meeting the Bowers and trying to understand not only the spoken but also the unspoken messages being sent among this group that would be his "family" for the next 10 months.

"Here we are," Mr. Bowers announced as their now silent carload drove into a small American town.

Huge houses lined well-paved streets. Trees shaded green lawns. "How many families live in one of those buildings?" Bold asked, his curiosity winning over his decision to remain quiet.

"Just one," Cammy answered, glad to have the silence broken at last.

"One? How many people in the family?" Bold's question escaped his lips before he realized it.

"It varies, but we live in a house like these."

Bold wished that he had maintained his vigilance of silence as he read the surprise in everyone's eyes. An overwhelming sense of being in over his head filled Bold, creating a heavy, muddy feeling. The Bowers' van pulled into the driveway of mansion-sized house surrounded by a yard that looked like a flawless carpet of green decorated with bright splashes of exotic gardens. Bold had never seen anything like it before, but he realized the Bower children had grown up surrounded by such opulence their entire lives. They would think he was just some kind of poor kid from the countryside if they saw the apartment he lived in with his family. In Zuunmod their home was considered palatial, but here it would seem grungy and much too small for the five of them.

The brothers helped Bold carry his bags into a room about the size of their living room in Zuunmod and left him to unpack. He sank onto the bed, unable to do anything more than soak in the many unique sights, sounds, smells and feelings that assaulted him. Ten long months stretched out before him. How would he ever survive?

# Chapter 3: New Routines Become Habits

"Bold, would you come help chop the lettuce for a salad?" Cheryl called from the kitchen a few days after his arrival.

Bold hesitated, frustration entering his gut as he pulled himself away from the TV show he had been lost in. *"Chop lettuce," what did that mean?* He had no idea. In Mongolia his sister had helped his mother in the kitchen, not him. Men worked outside, which meant that there wasn't as much to do for those living in the city. That had been fine with him. It gave him more time to relax in front of the TV or play basketball with friends.

Shaking the memories of the ease with which Bold and his friends had hanging out together, Bold dragged himself into the kitchen where Cheryl scampered around the room like a colt trying to avoid its trainer. *Where did the woman get so much energy?* Bold had never seen a group of people engage in so much activity that accomplished nothing when it came to meeting basic life needs. Their needs were met easily and quickly, and they chose to use the extra time earned to run around doing seemingly pointless tasks that took more effort than what they appeared to accomplish. For instance, Cammy and Michael both took piano lessons, for which they had to practice one hour each day. Michael and David played on different softball teams. They rushed off to practices by themselves, but everyone was expected to attend their games. Shopping could take an entire day if Cammy and Mrs. Bowers were in charge.

Despite the fact that Bold managed to avoid much of the insane activity they participated in, he still felt exhausted at the end of each day. He decided that simply being around it drank up the energy he used to direct toward schoolwork, chores and friends.

"Here, I'll show you what to do," Cheryl held a large knife in one hand, using the other hand to rhythmically push the blade through the head of lettuce. Her efficient movements made it look so easy.

Bold resented the assumption that he needed to be shown like a child how to do the task. He also resented being asked to do girl's work. Instead of soaking in the companionable silence that Cheryl offered, a dense fog of anger deadened his awareness of anything else.

As Bold scooped the last of the lettuce into the large yellow bowl, he planned his excuse to exit the room of humiliation before new torture could be conferred on him. But the entrance of Matt foiled his escape.

"Hey there, dinner smells great. Just a minute, and I'll wash up so I can help you two." He left, leaving behind an unspoken assumption that barred Bold's way.

Besides, Bold was too surprised to speak. Had Mr. Bowers just said he would help with dinner? Why? He had worked all day and should be relaxing in front of the TV by now. Mrs. Bowers did not work, and, even if she did, she should be getting him a drink and making sure he's comfortable. His own mother taught all day, and then hurried home to prepare dinner. What was going on here?

The fog of anger lifted and confusion mixed with curiosity settled on Bold as he waited to see just what Mr. Bowers meant when he promised to "help." Maybe he'd come back to sample the dinner and talk about his day. This Bold could understand.

"Hey, Bold, why aren't you with the boys? Where are Mike and David?" Mr. Bowers immediately zeroed in on Bold, clapping his shoulder with a gentleness that surprised Bold. It felt good, though, because in Mongolia men often hugged and touched each other. It allowed them to express friendship. Bold momentarily felt a connection that had not been felt since he boarded the plane for this new land.

As Mr. Bowers gave Mrs. Bowers a hug and kiss, however, Bold's sense of belonging faded into embarrassment because the open show of affection between a man and woman, even those married, was not considered appropriate in traditional families like his own. Bold struggled with such contradictions between the two cultures he now felt that he existed between.

Preoccupied with his own confused emotions, Bold forgot to respond to the question. Mr. Bowers' expectant look faded into acceptance, and he redirected his attention to his wife. "How was your day, honey?"

Bold felt relief and dismissal that tasted like the sweet and sour sauce they had with the meal the night before. The mixture didn't sit any better in his digestive system today than it had then. He opted for a silent retreat into more salad mixing. His mind hacked away at the true answer to Mr. Bower's question as to why Bold was not with the boys.

At first Bold had eagerly accepted their invitations to play basketball with their friends. He had changed into his favorite clothes—a jersey and matching shorts of bright blue and yellow color. The loose fit meant that the clothes seemed to soar with him as he flew around the basketball court. But no one else wore such flashy clothes. The other guys wore plain shorts and t-shirts, just like Michael and David. A few of them raised eyebrows when they saw him, but they politely refrained from commenting. Everyone that is, but Ryan.

Bold's cheeks burned as he remembered the sarcastic bite to Ryan's words, "Did you come to play basketball or to put on a circus act? I'll have to wear sunglasses to play on the same court as you." The others had laughed off Ryan's ridicule as they pushed Bold outside of the circle of conversation, shoving both Ryan's words and his disrespect away. Yet Bold knew that Ryan spoke what each one thought in his mind.

The next day Bold wore his alternative outfit for playing ball—jeans and a white t-shirt. Again, the sense of not being dressed quite right hit him as he saw everyone else in shorts. The humidity quickly drenched Bold in sweat, and the jeans, his only other choice besides the bright shorts, felt like weights attached to his legs. Returning to the basketball court would not be on his agenda this summer.

Bold felt at a loss not being able to play basketball with the guys. This was one place he could maneuver with confidence. Language rarely mattered. Bold could figure out what was expected and how he should respond by simply following the flow of the game. Possibly the court was the one place he could have built some friendships and made some connections, but the times between games and after, before the guys headed to their homes had been excruciatingly painful for Bold. They spoke quickly, using unfamiliar slang. If they allowed Bold to remain quiet, everything was fine, but as soon as they turned the conversation on him, he froze and looked away in shame.

To answer Mr. Bowers' question, Bold was not with the boys because he had feigned a headache so that he did not have to face the humiliation of not fitting in. Bold did not dress like them, and he did not talk like them. What else could he do but allow the boys to hang out with their friends, unimpeded by the stupid foreigner staying at their home?

A sudden quietness between the Bowers drew Bold's attention. He covertly glanced their way. Mr. Bowers' eyes looked worried as Mrs. Bower shrugged and patted his arm. What was that all about? It had to have been about him. Was he proving to be so difficult that they were considering sending him back already? Had he done something to offend them? Maybe they hadn't liked the fact that he had begged off of the game. How did they even know that he had declined the boys' offer?

"Here, I'll set the table," Mr. Bowers dispelled the uncomfortable atmosphere and began to gather dishes from the many cupboards lining the kitchen walls. Bold had been struck by the amount of storage space in the kitchen, wondering what they could possibly have to put into it. The overabundance of cooking utensils and food items amazed him. His family could eat for over two months just on the food in the Bowers' kitchen right then, and they could make a small fortune selling off all the extraneous pots, pans and gadgets.

Soon everyone was engaged with one task or another as the Bowers introduced Bold to meal preparation in America. Camaraderie settled on the group. Yet, Bold's pride still smarted from being made to do menial labor.

"Thanks, Bold," Mrs. Bowers' genuine appreciation cooled his temper with a realization that he had been a help.

The tumultuous entrance of David and Michael dispelled the warm moment. "What's for dinner?" Michael asked eagerly.

"Chicken pot pie," Cheryl responded.

"Ugh!" Michael tossed his enthusiasm down with his basketball, trudging off to wash his hands.

Bold felt embarrassed that Michael, who did not seem to even have noticed, had been so rude to his mother who had spent a lot of time making this meal. He saw a fleeting glimmer of hurt in her eyes, followed by a determined set of her shoulders and re-fixing of a smile on her face.

Without having acknowledged it before, Bold realized he had seen the same look on his mother's face when he had made similar comments.

Just then Cammy entered wearing a pink sweat suit and glowing smile. She slipped her hand into Bold's as she asked to sit by him during the meal. Ever since the first assault, Cammy had pulled back a little and yet never so far that Bold didn't know when she was around or that she wanted to be his friend.

"Don't forget that we're working on the yard tomorrow, guys." Mr. Bowers reminded the boys.

"Oh, dad, the guys are going to the river to swim tomorrow." Michael whined.

"Yeah, and we thought it would be a good idea to bring Bold. He hasn't seen the river yet." David persuasively added.

Bold immediately suspected that his presence was an afterthought, a way for the brothers to get out of doing yard work, whatever that was. He resented being used like this, remembering the relief that washed through David's eyes when he had claimed to have a headache earlier that day. But even stronger was the sense of panic that rode up this throat at the thought of swimming in a river. Beyond wading in a stream outside of Zuunmod, Bold had never been near a river, and he did not know how to swim. No way was he going to let the brothers and their friends see his ineptness.

"I'd like to help with the yard work, Mr. Bowers." Bold pushed the words past the bile sitting in the back of his throat. His dark eyes challenged the boys to try to use him any further in their plans.

"Sounds good. You can all go to the river after if there's time. With an extra set of strong hands, I'll bet we get done in no time." Mr. Bowers' grin at Bold calmed his stirring emotions.

"I guess," David conceded more readily than Michael who returned to his food in silence.

"May I go with them?" Cammy piped in, oblivious to the tension that sat like company at the table with them.

"Why not? We can all go," Cheryl forced out from behind her fixed smile.

Taking his cue, Matt agreed, "Sounds like a great idea. We can have a picnic."

"Yippee!" Cammy clapped her hands and settled back into her meal.

Bold silently began devising excuses he could use the next day when it came time to go to the river. For now he would leave the sense of unity in tact. He thought about how this provided yet another way that America differed so much from Mongolia.

In Mongolia "yard work" would have consisted of chopping wood , if any was available, for the stove, collecting dung, although this was considered women's work, seeing to the horses, sheep, goats, yaks, cows, and camels, or putting up the ger, a circular tent the herds-families lived in. Bold never imagined it meant collecting sticks that would not be burned, pushing a lawnmower to cut grass that would have been perfect for the animals to graze on, or pull weeds out of a garden. The stick collecting he could manage, despite its feeling like a girl's job. Why they didn't just run the lawn mower over the sticks was beyond Bold. But differentiating weeds from plants was impossible even after the parents and Cammy patiently tried to teach him.

The hot, humid air clung to Bold's skin. His jeans felt heavy, and his t-shirt felt like a wet towel hung over his shoulders. The men in the family worked with their shirts off, but Bold felt self-conscious in front of the women, so he left his on. Besides, he was dark enough and already stood out in this predominantly white town.

"I think we've done enough for today. Why doesn't everyone get cleaned up, put on their suits and meet by the car in 20 minutes?" Mr. Bowers ended the workday, looking at his wife for approval about the time.

Bold could not get used to the way Matt sought Cheryl's agreement. His father would never do that; it would mean that he was abandoning his role of master of his home. It would humiliate both himself and his wife. Cheryl usually agreed, so it was not really a big deal, but when she imperceptibly shook her head or raised her eyebrows, Matt would renege on his proffered plans and ask Cheryl what they should do instead. It did seem to work for them, but Bold knew that it would never fly where he came from.

"I don't have a suit," Bold blurted, hoping that would end his inclusion in this excursion.

Understanding lit Cheryl's eyes as she took in Bold's sweaty appearance. "Davey will have an old one that should fit you. Davey, why don't you get

Bold a swim suit as well as some shorts to wear. I know you have more than you need."

"Sure," David ran into the house to accomplish his mission.

Bold felt slapped in the face as the word 'charity' rang in his mind. Todd's lesson about helping out those 'less fortunate than oneself' had surprised Bold because he had been taught to help family no matter what, without judging who was better off. This could extend to close friends and neighbors as well. But to aid a stranger, even one living in the house, and to not expect anything in return was a foreign concept to him. Now here he was to become a charity case. He didn't need their pity or their clothes. He had brought plenty of good clothes; at least he had more than many boys his age in Zuunmod. Bold knew he would be expected to accept their cast offs and to appreciate the gesture, but a cold anger settled into his stomach as he entered the house to change.

By staying close to Cammy on the bank of the river, Bold avoided revealing his fear of the water. The river was deep with a slight current that would have overwhelmed him. Cammy enjoyed his company and readily included him in her building of sand castles.

After eating the picnic lunch, Michael and David quickly located their friends and disappeared until it was time to pack up and head home. Their noses and shoulders looked pink, and their tanning bodies glistened through the sheen of water covering them. They had had a wonderful day.

"Tomorrow we leave for church at 8:30. Breakfast will be at 8 for anyone interested," Matt proclaimed.

Bold knew these proclamations were for his benefit because the others obviously knew the schedule. But at least he wasn't singled out or left guessing what was next. He was glad he had his suit along. Bold had never been in a church before, but all the pictures he saw had men wearing suits.

The next morning Bold arrived at breakfast, satisfied that he would look just like everyone else that day. To his disappointment, the Bower boys wore casual shirts and pants. Cheryl tried to rescue him from drowning in his embarrassment with a compliment.

"You look nice, Bold."

"Thanks," he muttered as he stiffly sat with the others for breakfast.

"There's time if you want to change, Bold," Matt offered.

"No, that's okay," Bold's pride refused to let him admit total ignorance.

"Have you ever been to church?" Cammy asked innocently.

"I've been to the Buddhist temple in our town," he answered defensively.

"Wow," Cammy's big blue eyes pulled out Bold's frustration and replaced it with acceptance once again. "What is that like?"

"People just go to offer prayers. Their petitions are written on paper and stuck to a wheel that everyone turns as they pass by. There are also mats for people to lie on in supplication if they are really intense about something. But mostly people go to ask the Buddhist priests to say special prayers for them." Bold was thankful they had discussed religion with Todd so that he knew the right words to say.

"Well, our service lasts a lot longer, and it's not just about prayer," Michael instructed. "The pastor will go on and on about something we're supposed to do or not do."

"Michael," Matt interrupted his son's dissertation about church with a glint that expressed itself in his eyes and his voice. "You know that Christianity is not just about what we should and should not do. It's about a relationship with the Living God."

"Sorry. I just have a hard time sitting still for so long. I wish Pastor Kennedy would get to the point a lot faster." Michael slumped down in his chair.

Bold couldn't even begin to comprehend what Matt might mean about having a relationship with God, so he wondered instead about how he would be able to stay awake through a long lecture in English. Would he understand much of it? There would probably be many new words used. Would he know what to do, or would this be yet another opportunity to remind him just how much he did not belong here?

Once at church, Bold followed Cammy's lead so that he could sit and stand appropriately. The words to the songs were simple enough, so that he could sing along most of the time. The words were about a God who loved those whom he had created. There was even one about how this God sent His Son to die in the place of evil people. Bold wondered who these evil people were and whether or not they realized what had been done for them. He had to admit that there was a consistency here with what Todd had said to them in their home.

Bold discovered that by focusing on the pastor's huge nose, he could stay awake. He had noticed that Americans all had big noses, but this man's nose was gigantic. The pastor talked about the same loving God that they had sung about. Images of the Buddhist gods flashed into Bold's mind as he caught words here and there. What a different picture these Christians seemed to present of God. Bold thought about the altar, which contained a depiction of their family's god—a grotesque creature riding on a horse with humans hanging out of its greedy mouth, being consumed because of the evil they committed.

This use of fear to demand good behavior was the reason Bold's father rejected the Buddhist religion. He was not afraid of anything or anyone he often boasted. Bold's admiration for his father had drawn him to assert the same beliefs, but deep down inside Bold was afraid. He was afraid he would shame his family, lose his father's respect, or that he would fail and not become the great success his family was counting on him to become.

Besides, as he watched his mother perform her Buddhist traditions and listened to her talk about the need to treat others with kindness, Bold knew there was much more to Buddhism than the family god. It was just that his mother seemed so alone in her spiritual life, and she still had to work awfully hard to make sure that she would have success after she died.

Such pressure did not seem to exist for David, Michael or Cammy. Even Cheryl and Matt Bowers did not seem to get caught up in what others thought of them. They seemed to be so comfortable with who they were and what they would do next. What would it be like to live life free of the burden of being perfect?

Bold's musings lasted until the end of the service. They did not prepare him for what came next, however—Sunday school. David led him down a hall to a classroom filled with other teenagers. After dutifully introducing Bold around, David became engaged in conversation with a group of the boys. They openly included Bold but did not insist that he respond after the initial inquiries made out of politeness. Evidently David had filled them in, so this newcomer did not arouse their curiosity. Bold relaxed, realizing that the taunting challenge he had felt during the two times playing basketball in the neighborhood did not exist in this circle of guys.

The teacher turned out to be a young girl who didn't seem to be much older than the students. Bold fully expected the boys in the class to act up and possibly even flirt with her, but that did not happen. They eagerly listened to what she had to say about a book called the Bible. When she asked a question, they politely raised their hands, waiting to be acknowledged before answering. They not only seemed to know what she was talking about, but they seemed to care about it and to even believe it. Bold tried to understand as much as possible, feeling that here might be the key to fitting into this strange new world. But the ideas presented were antithetical to the way Bold saw life. Even the American TV channel—MTV—did not agree with these values espoused as so crucial to living a good life.

Bold finally tired of trying to comprehend the seeming contradictions. If someone really did live by the standards presented in this class, he would be walked all over and would never get ahead in life. It just wouldn't work. Maybe someone could do it here in America, but never in Mongolia.

The mental exhaustion of trying to interpret the morning's happenings made it hard for Bold to keep his eyes open through Sunday dinner. He excused himself after and surrendered fully to a deep slumber. This had not been a day of rest for him.

# Chapter 4: Stepping Out

Bold hesitated as he reached out his arm toward the door leading into the grocery store. He wasn't sure if this one would automatically open up or not. Being hit by a door that operated on its own was not the type of experience he had come to America for. Even after two and a half weeks, he still felt like an outsider and a klutz.

He remembered how startled he had been the first time his host family had taken him to a store with automatic doors. He had stumbled backwards, almost falling, and they had laughed at his surprise with that superiority mixed with kindness that made him feel so foolish. His sun-browned cheeks burned red even now as he thought about it. The fact everyone could always see his shame despite his efforts to be stoic at all times added fuel to the slow burning anger that seemed to have arrived with him the same day his plane landed in America.

This door required Bold to push it open. The first obstacle had been successfully navigated in this course set by his host mom when she asked him to "pick up a few things" at the store for her. She had no idea how panic coursed through Bold as these innocuous words spilled out of her mouth. She was asking him to negotiate in a world that confused him terribly.

Once inside, Bold did not let his guard down. He knew that he faced one of the greatest challenges of this adventure—finding and deciding on what to buy. Tall aisles filled with every food imaginable imperiously dared him to discover the listed items they kept securely hidden amidst many other things that looked similar but were not needed.

A cart would be required, for despite her request for a "few things" Bold knew from the list that it contained more items than he had ever before gone shopping for at one time. When he went with Cheryl on her weekly shopping trip, he could not believe the amount of food she piled into the cart.

Nor could he fathom the fact that the food was consumed throughout the week so that more was soon needed. How could a family of five eat so much?

As he wrenched the cart from the stack, he stepped back, crunching a foot under his own and making contact with a stranger. Reflexively, Bold's hand flew back to grasp the unknown person's hand, a tradition that re-established broken relationships immediately where he came from. He remembered where he was too late and apologized into the startled face of an older woman who clutched her purse tightly to her chest.

"I'm so sorry. I did not know you were behind me. Please forgive my clumsiness," he gushed, hoping words would make it all right and that his cheeks would not stay red the entire time he was in the store. His hooded eyes conveyed humble contrition and hid smoldering anger that he had let himself forget where he was.

"I should think you would be, young man," she huffed as she grabbed a cart and aggressively forced it into the section of fresh fruits and vegetables.

Bold had studied the list during the three blocks to the store, so he did not need to check it again. He thought he could identify each item and match it to what he had seen Cheryl use in the kitchen when he helped her cook. His observation skills were being honed as he watched everything people did, trying to mimic mannerisms, so it would not be so obvious that he did not belong here. Many times people asked him to do things they simply assumed he knew how to do, and he hated having to admit his ignorance, so as often as possible, he took his cues from others and improvised the rest.

The heat that had almost receded from his cheeks now flared up again, giving them a sunburned look. After almost three weeks, Bold finally felt comfortable helping in the kitchen, something that had always been his older sister's job. Yet, anyone around at the time of meal preparation was asked to help, even Mr. Bowers, so Bold swallowed his angst and did as he was asked.

He was thankful that the program encouraged the students to arrive in August, before school began. Bold had found adapting to life with the Bowers confusing enough without adding the stress of trying to make it in a new school. That would come soon enough.

Focus. That's what he needed to do if he was to have any hope of accomplishing this assignment before the food was needed. He decided to take one aisle at a time, scanning for the items as he slowly navigated the obstacle course set by other shoppers and their carts. He quickly developed a headache as his mind had so many details to concentrate on all at once. His preference would have been to walk through the entire store, looking for one item at a time, but the store was too big for that, so his mind raced as he pictured each item and looked for its twin on the over-packed shelves before him.

Occasionally, Bold recognized a section by the name on the aisle's label and could either quickly move on, knowing it contained nothing he needed or could stop and look for a specific item he knew existed in that place. Then he had to decide which of the many similar looking products was the one Mrs. Bowers really wanted. Such choices did not exist in the stores back home, so Bold's mind revolted, and he had to force it to remember the tiniest details from what he had seen in Cheryl's kitchen. Then he would grab what he thought was the closest thing, drop it into the cart and move quickly away, hoping his indecision had not been obvious to others. This constantly being on display, and feeling watched and judged unsettled Bold more than anything. At home he loved it when people paid attention to him, but here he wanted nothing more than to blend in; something he would never be able to do.

"May I help you, sir?" A boy about his age dressed in jeans and a blue vest stopped placing boxes of cereal on shelves and looked at Bold with a sincere desire to help him. But Bold did not even know how to pronounce the name of the cereal, which Cammy loved to eat every morning. He just knew that the box was pink and had a rabbit on it. The section of cereals was five shelves high and seemed to be a block long. It didn't help matters that several were brightly colored and carried images of cute animals. Bold contemplated walking away right then, but knew that he couldn't return home without Cammy's cereal. She had finished it that morning.

"Yes, please. I am looking for this cereal," Bold pointed to the brand name on the list.

"That's right over here," the red haired boy grinned, walked to a shelf, pulled off the box Bold was looking for, tossed it into Bold's cart and resumed his task of stocking shelves.

"Thanks," Bold grinned at the boy's chest and then into hazel eyes that genuinely did not appear to mind helping this foreigner. He did not seem to look at Bold as someone who didn't belong there or someone who was a bother. With relief and hope, Bold headed for the next aisle, filled with snack foods.

"Young man, could you move your cart, please?" The elderly woman shoved at Bold's cart with her own, a temporary warrior instinct rose up inside of him, but Bold managed to reign it in before responding.

"Sure, sorry."

"You should be." She sputtered under her breath as she charged down the aisle.

Bold realized that she had had plenty of room to go around him but had chosen to boss him around instead. Despite her age and his upbringing to respect everyone older than himself, Bold's previous sense of wellbeing evaporated into a bitter air of resentment.

"Excuse me, do you work here? You seem to be spending a lot of time in one place. Could you help me find the sugar-free section?" The elderly man appeared confused, mirroring Bold's own perception of trying to shop there.

"I'm sorry, I do not work here." Bold's automatic desire to help this fragile gentleman was squelched by the knowledge that he had no idea where the "sugar-free section" was or how to find it. "I am not sure where anything is." The apology stuck in his throat, making Bold aware of how dry his mouth had become during this adventure of terror. As he swallowed his regrets, they settled in his gut with the many other emotions that he had been forced to eat that day.

"That's okay. Thanks anyway." The man walked away. Bold then thought he heard the man wheeze, "Stupid, Mexicans."

What did that mean? Did the man think Bold was a Mexican? And why did the man express such contempt when he said it? A chill ran down Bold's spine as he continued his search for the chocolate chip cookies that the boys consumed in volumes between meals.

Bold moved stiffly up and down the remaining aisles in a daze. After an hour of painstaking decision-making and humiliating offers of help by customers who noticed his various dilemmas, Bold approached the row of cashiers. His legs trembled, needing encouragement to move forward. He felt in his pocket for the money Mrs. Bowers had given him. He had no idea how much the 10 items would cost, and he hoped he had enough to cover it all.

Everything in America cost so much more. At home Bold had felt rich, knowing that his cousins had many animals in their herds so his family would never go hungry. He had always worn clothes that looked like the people on MTV, a favorite show. His parents both worked and were highly respected in Zuunmod, but here no one knew his family. His clothes, which had been more than enough before, barely filled two drawers, while the two boys in the family had two dressers each, as well as large closets, filled with clothes. They eagerly gave Bold whatever he needed, but their kindness always seemed tainted by the mutual knowledge that they gave out of their abundance to someone who did not have enough.

How had he gone from thinking about food to clothes? Bold knew these thoughts had a well-worn path in his mind these days. The ruts filled with discontent and frustration at feeling that he was not on equal terms with these people who graciously opened their home to him. Sure, they never put him down, and their laughter at his mistakes sounded good-natured and was probably meant to make him feel comfortable, but he was not a charity case. He decided that this must be exactly how they viewed him, and after that he withdrew into a polite indifference and stiffness that allowed him live in their home without being drawn into their hearts.

"Do you have any coupons?" the clerk asked without looking up, pushing buttons on the register.

"No," he responded, hoping it was the right answer. He remembered Mrs. Bowers teaching him about coupons as she sat at the kitchen table clipping squares out of the newspaper.

"Okay," she sighed, efficiently moving his items before a scanner that threw numbers on the screen in front of her. The speed and electronic pinging always made Bold anxious; it was as if something irrevocable was happening that would trap him forever.

"The total is $26.79." She finally made eye contact as her hand expressed its desire for the money he held.

Panic took over. Bold handed her all three 20-dollar bills that he had. Flames lit up his face as she sighed, more loudly this time, took two bills and handed him back the third. He covered his shame by stuffing the bill into his pocket and moving to the end of the counter to bag his groceries.

"Here's your change," she placed the money on the belt and began serving the next person in line.

Without saying another word, Bold hurried to the door with his two bags out the door, reaching to push it open and finding himself stumbling a bit as it opened by itself. He cursed in his native tongue and headed towards "home."

As soon as the word "home" plopped into his mind, Bold realized that this was the one decision he had been refusing to make. He thought he needed to protect himself and to maintain his dignity at all costs. The others had sensed his desire to remain aloof and had drawn back as well. The boys no longer asked Bold if he wanted to go with them and their friends to movies or bike riding. They played basketball every afternoon, a game Bold used to love, but he had systematically refused to join them until they stopped asking.

As he passed the park where they played he saw them with their friends. Both stopped playing basketball and waved as he walked by. Their smiles held no condescension or anger at him. Bold responded with an awkward wave and a smile that unconsciously reflected their openness towards him. For the first time that day something other than anger, fear or embarrassment ran down the back of his throat and brought the redness to his cheeks. It was hope.

A modern hip-hop song by Bold's favorite group rang through his head as he approached the Bowers' home. As he hurried up the driveway, he noted that Matt's car was back from work. He hoped that he had not taken too long.

Removing his shoes just inside the front door, Bold heard voices in the kitchen. Mr. and Mrs. Bowers were having a serious discussion about something.

"I just don't know if it's working out, Matt. He doesn't seem to be happy. I don't even think he likes us." Cheryl's voice held unshed tears.

"I don't understand it either, honey. I think we've been accepting and welcoming. Maybe he comes from a place that takes life more seriously. Maybe he is happy but does not express it like we do. We're trying something new." His voice betrayed the fact that even he did not believe his words.

"Well then, why doesn't he go with the boys and their friends? What are we doing wrong? He hardly does anything; all day he sits in the family room watching TV, and sometimes he plays a game with Cammy. She seems to be the only one who can draw him out."

"We knew this wasn't going to be easy. It takes time to bring someone into a new family, into a new country. Bold has a lot of adjustments to make. I think the best we can do is pray about it and wait. Let's let him decide how involved he wants to be with us. We can't force relationships on another person."

"I know you're right. I just get impatient and feel like such a failure. Besides, it's not always fun to be around such a sullen person. I feel as though I'm walking on eggshells around him." Cheryl's sigh pierced Bold's heart as he realized what a problem he really was for this family.

Why couldn't he get it right? Why couldn't he just relax and fit in, become the person they wanted him to be? She wasn't the failure; he was. As the thoughts shot through his mind, though, a black rage engulfed his heart. Why should he have to change himself just to make these people happy? Had they really tried to understand who he was or where he had come from? Sure they asked questions, but at those times Bold felt like he was being interrogated and that he had to defend himself and his country. They seemed to only be curious about what made him different, what made him inferior. Bold did not understand the origin of so much anger inside of him, but it had taken up residence in his heart ever since he began life in this new place.

Bold felt the bags collapsing under his tight grip and knew that he'd better get them into the kitchen before he destroyed what had taken so much time and effort to acquire. Coughing to announce his arrival, Bold pushed into the kitchen, keeping his defiant eyes down as he plopped the bags on the counter, dug the change out of his pocket and placed it beside the bags, and left without a word.

"You don't suppose he heard us, do you?" a worried Matt asked his wife.

"I don't know. That's just the way he is sometimes." Cheryl tried to shrug it off, denying that their words might have had an impact on their guest.

# Chapter 5: Beginning to See with New Eyes

"Bold, are you ready to go?" Cheryl called up the stairs as she grabbed her purse and gave Matt the "eye" to turn off the news and come too.

"Yes." The oddity of having something special for him to attend with Mr. and Mrs. Bowers settled in Bold's stomach like a huge ball that emitted thick gas that had to be swallowed down every few seconds. What would be expected of him tonight? Who would be there? Why did they even have to go? Weren't they doing fine? Were there problems that the Bowers would bring up, putting Bold on the spot; maybe even demanding that the organization take him back and find him another home?

Cheryl's encouraging smile laid to rest some of his queries, but a nagging sense of doom continued to buzz in his ear. Matt entered the front hall just as Bold did, keeping the progression towards the car moving. "Are you excited to meet other exchange students, Bold?"

"Sure," he produced the correct answer without considering, or even caring about, its veracity.

With the radio tuned to a Christian music and news station, everyone settled into silence. It was companionable for the Bowers and protective for Bold. He did not even enter into dialogue with himself, imposing a strict, stony silence of avoidance. They would arrive at the school and then would be time enough to think, to feel and to respond. One thing he had learned so far in his time in America was that there was no way to prepare for the unknown.

"It looks like it'll be a full room. I'll drop you off and find a spot." Matt offered. Bold wished that he had the guts to ask if he could stay with Matt, but he knew that this was all for him and that he had to play his part responsibly.

"Thanks, dear," Cheryl hopped out, waiting for Bold to join her. Then, linking arms with him, she led the way to the school's cafeteria. "I hope you can meet some people who will be in class with you, Bold. It's not easy being the new kid in school. Friends always make it easier. Of course, you'll have David here, too. I'm sure he'll help you with anything you need help with." Her voice faltered, registering the fact that she had noticed that Bold and David were not very close. They rarely spent time together and barely spoke during meals or other family events.

Wanting to distract the condemnation he knew she must be feeling towards him at that moment, Bold spoke reassuringly, "I'm sure there will be many people here who will be in my classes. That will be nice."

Bold would have been able to find the cafeteria on his own by simply following the noise in the otherwise silent school. The emptiness felt ominous, and the size made him feel very small. A spark of defensive anger lit in the depths of his heart as he realized how little he knew about attending school in America.

"Welcome, please find your name tags and take a folder." A person whose tag read "Hostess" channeled Bold and Cheryl down a table covered with paraphernalia. Before they knew it, they were inside the doors of the cafeteria, looking at a sea of faces that held a variety of shades of color. The atmosphere was electrical, as if some great announcement was about to be made. Only Cheryl's eager and compelling presence next to him kept Bold from exiting immediately. This was no place for him; of that he was sure.

"Wow, I had no idea so many families were involved. Let's find some seats at a table. Then if you want to mingle, you can."

Bold followed obediently, stopping to wait when Cheryl greeted the many parents that she knew. Once he captured a chair, he did not want to leave it. He just wanted to observe and try to understand. At the table next to theirs a couple sat squabbling about whose fault it was that their real son was failing math. The Chinese student with them sat bored, trying to catch Bold's eye. Bold judiciously avoided the boy, recalling the stories of Chinese he had heard back home. They were dirty people who were not to be trusted. This boy was definitely someone he would have to keep at a distance.

With that thought, Bold turned in his chair and focused on those sitting at the same table as him. Just as he adjusted his chair inward, a voice forced him to take notice. "Hi, my name is Romero." The boy's eyes danced out to capture Bold's attention, and his smile brought one to Bold's lips along with a response.

"Hi, I'm Bold. Where are you from, Romero?"

"Venezuela. How about you, Bold? That's a great name, by the way."

"Thanks. I'm from Mongolia."

"Wow! You're a long way from home, aren't you?"

"Aren't we all?" Bold deflected, stuffing down the wave of homesickness threatening to drown him as it had so many times before.

"Yeah, I guess. What grade are you in, Bold?"

"It's the 11th grade in Mongolia, which would have been my last year. I'm not sure where they'll put me here. How about you?" Bold felt good that he could use some of the slang and conversation short cuts he had picked up at the Bowers'.

"I 11th grade, also." The error rang in Bold's ear, and he searched Romero's face to see if this boy from Venezuela cared. All he saw was an invitation to be friends. Bold's instincts told him to hold back, to be cautious, because a friendship that was so easily offered would usually cost him much in the end.

"Nice to meet you. If you'll excuse me, I have to go . . ." Bold had no real place to go. He didn't even really know where he was, so he left the sentence unfinished between them and slid towards the door they had entered through. He kept his eyes down, hoping that Romero would not be offended but also would not assume that they were to be great friends.

Bold was not sure he wanted friends in this country anyway. No one could replace his friends back home who knew him so well and could be trusted with his life. A sigh expressed his nostalgia just as Matt Bowers made his entrance.

"Hi, Bold. Did you find good seats? Do you need help with anything?"

As he pointed to the seats where Cheryl sat as queen of the conversation, Bold gave the excuse he had come to depend on quite a bit lately. "No, I was just stretching my legs."

"Okay, don't go too far; I think they're going to start soon. You won't want to miss anything. This is just for you, you know." Matt's gentle pat on Bold's shoulder and gentle tone tugged at the tarp covering Bold's heart. He wished that he could relax and return the sentiment, but he didn't know how, and it felt so false to express emotions that were so foreign to him.

"I won't. I'll just be a minute." Bold assured him, shrugging the tarp back into place and moving towards the front doors. He knew he should just go back in with Matt, but something in him refused to allow him to acquiesce. Every time Bold considered changing direction and joining in the life of the Bowers, an instinctive urge compelled him to continue forward on the path he had already planned out for himself. He could not let go and join life in America. Maybe his gut knew something he didn't as to the true cost of becoming a part of what he saw around him.

After about thirty seconds of standing outside the front entryway, Bold sauntered back to the table, rejoining the group and reminding himself not to give too much attention to Romero, or the Chinese kid at the next table, for that matter. He decided to check out the girls instead. A Japanese girl at the table in front of them hijacked his attention. She had a mod look and seemed distant from everything and everyone around her. She almost appeared to be of royal blood and yet very down to earth and real, too.

Romero, following Bold's eyes, also saw her. "Hey, where you think she's from? She's not Mongolian, too, is she?"

Bold's mask slipped and temporarily revealed his contempt for Romero whose English was not very good. "No, I'm sure she's from Japan."

"She looks like snob, maybe. What you think?"

"Probably," Bold just wanted the conversation to end. However, no matter what signals he sent, Romero did not seem to get the hint. It was as if he had already decided that he and Bold would be friends. As Bold dragged his eyes from Romero to look anywhere else, hoping to further indicate his lack of interest, they landed on Romero's host parents.

Bold had never seen such tired looking people. Actually, he had, in Mongolia, but they were people tired after putting up a ger or sheering their herd or doing some kind of true physical labor. In America he did not see people who looked truly exhausted. They looked frazzled (a new word he had read just that morning) and deceptively tired from running in circles all day, but never as though they had just accomplished some labor of worthwhile exertion. As he thought about it, he had to admit that David and Michael sometimes came close after playing basketball with their friends, but even they usually quit before they hit the zenith of their energy.

This couple, though, looked exhausted—physically and emotionally. Bold couldn't help looking back at Romero, who had noticed Bold's examination of his surrogate family and slightly nodded that what Bold was thinking was accurate. Romero was not in a good home. This drew Bold's attention back to the Chinese kid at the next table whose parents were still bickering quietly. He still looked bored and miserable, not even trying to connect with anyone around him. Maybe Bold's rebuff had defined his situation for him all too plainly.

The boy jerked slightly and raised his eyes to Bold's. The pleading look demanded a response and forced Bold to choose—his ingrained prejudice against the Chinese or compassion for someone in a far worse situation than his. Until this moment many of Bold's decisions had been rather self-concerned, so he seriously considered sneering at the boy or even flipping him off, but the days of isolation cautioned Bold against sealing his fate so permanently. This thought was reinforced when he realized that not only Romero, but also the Japanese girl, seemed to be watching his exchange with the Chinese boy. He would be accepting or rejecting them as well.

Bold met the boys' eyes with the pride of Ghengis Khan and then rolled them at the bickering couple. The Chinese boy smiled, nodded and shrugged to indicate that their ridiculous behavior was a constant event. Bold's face then broke into a real grin that cemented their friendship. When he glanced at Romero and the Japanese girl, his grin still in place, he discovered that somehow an alliance had been formed. He would have friends when he started school in September, whether he had wanted to or not.

Before he could begin to worry about whether or not he had made a mistake, a bald man with an officious air about him began to address the group. He told them that the first order of business would be to have the students introduce themselves and tell their country of origin. Bold panicked, not wanting to be put on the spot in front of so many strangers. Fortunately, they were sitting towards the back, so it would be a while before they even got to him. Maybe he could "stretch his legs" again. As if reading his mind, Cheryl's hand gently attached itself to his arm.

Usually a gesture like this would offend Bold and begin the boiling of his anger, but tonight, after seeing so many different family situations and what he could have been stuck with, he acknowledged it for what it was—kind concern. Without indicating that he even felt the touch, Bold relaxed and tried to focus on the people introducing themselves. Ikota was the Japanese girl's name, and the Chinese boy was Wang. Those were the only two names he would try to remember tonight.

"My name is Romero, and I am from Venezuela."

This cued Bold to stand and introduce himself. He could not remember what he said or if it made sense, but the reassuring smile on Matt's face seemed to say that he had done okay. Bold cast a glance at Ikota's set of parents and noticed that the stiffness he had noticed in her seemed to run in the family. Maybe she was simply adjusting herself to those with whom she was living. He would have to find out.

Bold began to reflect on what made Cheryl and Matt Bowers unique. He admitted to himself that he never felt threatened or put down by them. They encouraged each other, their children and Bold regularly. When they got angry or said something cruel or hurtful, they always apologized soon afterward. They didn't make excuses for their behavior either; they admitted it had been wrong and that they should not have done it. The Bowers actually seemed to like each other, too. They spent time together, teased each other and helped each other out whenever someone needed it.

Just as Bold was about to identify what made them so different, even from many families he knew in Mongolia, the speaker in front raised his voice and intruded on Bold's thoughts. "And so, if you will help yourself to a piece of pie and greet at least three new people, we'll call it a night. Thank you."

"Come on, Bold; let's get some pie." Romero hurried Bold away, grabbing Wang on the way to the table. Actually he seemed to be taking a circuitous route to the desert table, making Bold wonder if he knew where they were supposed to be going. Just as he was about to correct his new friends, Bold caught sight of their real destination—Ikota.

"Hi, Ikota, right?" Romero held out his hand to a relieved looking Ikota who gladly shook it. She was standing with a Korean girl.

"Right. Romero, Wang and Bold." She looked for affirmation, but it was obvious she needed none. Remembering names seemed to be one of her talents. She might turn out to be a real asset in this place with hundreds of students. "This is Sheila. She'll have to tell you her Korean name; I don't have the pronunciation quite right yet, but I will."

"Pleased to meet you," the shy, petite girl said with a timorous smile, which seemed even more wavering next to Ikota's confidence.

Wang eagerly shook hands with both girls and then stepped aside as Bold took his turn. Ikota's eyes were bold and direct, reminding him of Saraa's. But the comparison ended there. Only Saraa would ever make his heart soar. That was good to know. It established some ideas for Bold that would make this friendship much easier. Sheila reminded him of his younger sister, someone needing his protection.

"Let's get pie," Romero herded them to the table. He began entertaining them with a story about his grandmother's berry pie, which was the best thing this side of "Heaven."

"Are you a Christian?" Ikota asked, interrupting the flow of his story, but not throwing Romero off at all.

"Yes, a Catholic. My family's ties to the Catholic Church go way back. I think I'm the 6th generation. What about you?"

"Yes, but I am the first generation. My parents do not believe. I hope that here in America I can learn more. It is difficult for me to attend church or practice Christianity in my family that is Buddhist." Ikota's face held a mixture of glowing hope and regretful fatalism.

"Buddhism, that is my family's religion also. I am a Buddhist and have not been able to find out about the Buddhist temple here." Sheila shocked everyone by speaking so much and about something so personal. Her desire became all the more real to them in what it must have cost her to enter the conversation.

"I can ask Cheryl about it." Bold wondered at this offer. Cheryl and Matt were Christians, not Buddhists. Why would they know about the temple? Yet, the fact they were Christians seemed to be the very reason that they might help Sheila. But just in case, he added, "I don't know if they'll know anything, but I'll ask."

Wang pushed his way into the conversation next, eyes flashing with annoyance mixed with some fear of rejection, "I am an atheist. Chinese people do not believe in God. He is a myth created by those wanting power over the weak minded."

Tension flared up, dividing people who had just a moment earlier been united in the determination to make the most of their new experience and to help each other survive. Romero quickly diffused it as he put his arm around Wang's shoulder and handed him a piece of pie from the table, "Well, Wang, then I guess I'm weak minded and will need help with homework. What you think? Pie?" His comical grin communicated that he did not think himself stupid at all, and everyone laughed.

Wang good-naturedly, and with seeming relief, accepted the pie and handed Romero one. "Here, let's eat pie." The others grabbed their own pieces and headed to a table in the corner where they could eat and chat, knowing that this would establish relationships that they would need in the weeks ahead.

At one point the conversation turned to their host families. "My family constantly argues. I think they hate each other. If my mother spoke the way Mrs. Morrison does to her husband, my father would beat her and send her back to her family in disgrace. It is horribly noisy and uncomfortable."

"Do they have any children of their own?" Sheila asked.

"Yes, one son who is never home. He is part of a band and always gone, practicing, so he says. I think he and his friends just smoke marijuana and run the streets. He sure is lucky, but I don't want to hang out with him and his friends. I'd probably get into trouble and be sent home." Wang sighed and slumped into a mound of self-pity.

"Well, my family doesn't argue all of the time; they don't talk at all. I've never lived in a more silent house. It's like a morgue! They speak to each other as if they are polite strangers. 'Please pass me the butter, dear.' 'Here you are, dear.' 'Thank you, dear.' And that will be the entire dinner conversation." Ikota's imitation of her host parents made everyone laugh. Her ability to mimic others would prove to be quite entertaining in the following months. But frustration also rang out of her words, and others cut off their laughter to murmur their condolences.

"The Garcias never stop talking. I feel like I'm living in a circus and would love a moment of polite silence." Sheila added her complaints, showing that she would be part of this group and needed to express herself as much as they did.

"That sounds like my family in Venezuela. Aunts, uncles, grandparents, brothers, sisters, everyone is always coming and going, talking and laughing. There always is a crowd. I never feel alone there, but here I have much time on my hands. I do not like to speak to my host family because they laugh at my poor English. They always put each other down, too. I think it way they express their love each other, but it sounds more like hate to me, and I don't think they be happy really."

Bold felt momentarily guilty that he had thought less of Romero for his mistakes in English and determined that he would not let himself think that way again. Brushing away his guilt, he joined in, unsure how to express his own experience. "Well, I have an okay family, the Bowers. They are nice people and have tried to welcome me. After hearing about your families, I feel lucky, but they still don't seem to understand me or what it's like coming to America for the first time. I get so angry sometimes and want to break something. In little ways they make me feel stupid and like an outsider. But I should be thankful that they are not like the Morrisons who fight all of the time. I could not live with that." He gave Wang a sympathetic look and then looked at the floor, feeling as if he had somehow betrayed the Bowers by complaining about them.

Ikota seemed to feel the same prick of conscience because she changed the subject to what classes they would be taking. They were all relieved that at least one other person in their group would be with them in each class. They agreed to meet by the front doors the first morning and to eat lunch together. Maybe that first day would not be quite so daunting.

"So, how was it, Bold? It looks like you've already made some friends." Cheryl beamed at him, appearing to be truly happy and relieved.

"Yes, I have met some nice people here. I think that next week will not be so bad."

"Good. Friends always make new experience more fun and less scary," Matt contributed from the drivers' seat. From there Matt and Cheryl began discussing some details for the next week. Bold sank back, happy to not have to converse. It had been a good night after all.

# Chapter 6:
# More New Experiences

The small alarm clock buzzed persistently, dragging a resisting Bold out of dreams about home. He remembered with a jolt that he was not home, he was now in America and that today was the first day of school. With a rush of adrenaline, he shot out of bed and headed for the shower. He had carefully listened to the morning plans of the others and had set his alarm for a half hour before anyone was going to get up. Bold had wanted to be sure to get a shower and have extra time to get ready for the first day of school.

As the hot water massaged his body more awake, Bold thought about the first day of school last year, when he had been home in Zuunmod. The night before that day he had been out late playing basketball with his friends, so he had stumbled through the morning routine, finally opening his eyes as he walked out the door. Instead of asking his mom to iron his school clothes, he had neatly placed them between his mattresses, pressing them as he slept. Since he saw his friends all of the time anyway, he did not really look forward to school, where teachers and school work would interfere with his socializing. At the same time, he knew that it was his next to last year and that he had nothing to fear, so he had strode through the school doors with confidence.

This year was different. He was not sure what to expect and wondered how others would respond to this new kid from Mongolia. He already dreaded having to introduce himself and to explain exactly where Mongolia was. Cammy had asked him enough questions already to cue him on the many misconceptions Americans had about his home country. He had also carefully watched the Bowers boys' faces when he talked about life in Mongolia, observing that many things that were "normal" to Bold were considered strange and even funny by them. Keeping a low profile was his goal for the day. He just wanted to sit back and observe. Participation was not a requirement. At least he had some friends who would be there, experiencing the same things.

"Bold, you look great!" Cheryl, obviously, thought his confidence needed boosting. Her voice rang with false cheerfulness.

"Thank you," Bold self-consciously focused on the food arranged on the table for breakfast. He began to wonder if he had chosen the right outfit, which consisted of blue jeans and a white with green and blue stripes polo shirt, but felt relief when David walked in wearing similar clothes. This more casual approach to school would take some getting used to for Bold.

"Hey," David greeted the room in general. "This looks great, mom."

"Well, I couldn't let you start the first day of school without a good breakfast, now could I?"

Suddenly, Bold's stomach clutched, and he wondered if he would be able to eat anything. Breakfast was not a priority in his family, so he often just rolled out of bed and hurried off to school. Yet, to not eat anything would be rude. Cheryl had gone to a lot of trouble for them. Forcing himself to slowly consume eggs, sausage and toast, Bold used eating to hide the intense emotions churning inside of him. The heat that raised it to boiling and seemed to keep it moving was anger. He would not let anyone make a fool of him today. Defiance welled up and dominated the other emotions. It darkened his eyes and clenched his jaw in such a way that would ward off all others—friends or foes.

As Bold stoically took the last minute instructions from Cheryl before heading out with David to the bus, he realized his resolve confused her. She reached out and leaned forward as if to hug him goodbye, but then stopped herself and withdrew, patting his shoulder instead. The warmth from her hand stayed with Bold as he waited for the bus, making him wonder if a hug would not have been even better. Yet, it might have destroyed him, too. He had to maintain control if he was to make it through today and not ruin his time in America.

Getting on the bus, Bold felt the person behind him step on his heel. Without thinking, Bold reached behind to grab the person's hand. The boy shoved Bold, causing him to stumble up the last step, irritated at Bold's slight hesitation and not even noticing his extended hand. Bold's heart lurched forward with his body as he realized that grabbing the boy's hand would have been even worse. He had to keep his attention focused at all times. Actions that were automatic at home would be misconstrued as ridiculous, or even offensive, here.

"Bold, sit here," David stood and let Bold sit by the window.

"Thanks," Bold mumbled, truly relieved not to have to sort out where he should sit on the bus already packed with students.

"No problem," David met Bold's eyes with open friendship, but Bold could not respond. He turned to look out the window after a smile that played only across his lips. He hoped he hadn't hurt David's feelings and relaxed when he felt David shift in the seat and begin talking to the boy across the aisle. David was probably just as happy not to have to try and think of anything to say.

Envy that David had his friends and his reputation to give him confidence this first day of school bit into Bold's gut. Wondering what his own friends were doing right then, Bold settled into a discontented reverie of past school days spent with people who knew and liked him.

Gratitude for an inside seat temporarily washed away the bitterness seething inside. "Bold, I'll see you around," David threw over his shoulder as he exited surrounded by friends. Bold sat back and waited for the bus to empty, taking his time to regroup his emotions and focus his attention.

The variety of people amazed Bold. Contempt rose into his heart as he noticed the obvious wealth represented by the students. They all appeared to be trying to express themselves with clothes that held little character. One girl with a Mohawk and several piercings stomped out of her father's car, her face lighting up when she saw two others with similar black clothes, heavy boots and dog collars on. Then they turned as a single unit of identity, set their faces with hard looks and strode into school, acting like they were about to fight a great battle.

Bold entered just behind the trio, hoping that Ikota, Romero, Sheila or Wang would have arrived first. He did not want to stand around waiting alone. He had never felt so self-conscious or overwhelmed before in his life. How were all of these students going to be organized and successfully taught here? Sure, the school was three times the size of his in Zuunmod, but everyone seemed to be crowded together in the front entryway, and more and more buses drove up, dumping off students.

"Hey, what are you, a freaking tourist? Look where you're going." A big kid with a blue and gold jacket shoved Bold out of his way. Anger leaped to his heart, and his fists knotted up, ready to respond. But the boy was already several steps away, greeting others with the same jacket. Bold was forgotten as quickly as he had been intruded upon. He did not know which was worse, though. Fortunately, he did not have long to think about it.

"Hey, Bold, over here!" Sheila and Wang stood off to the left of the main doors. They huddled together and looked as relieved to see Bold as he was to see them. Seeing Sheila reminded him that he had forgotten to ask Cheryl about a Buddhist temple in the area. He'd have to remember that tonight for sure.

"Hey! How are you? This is quite the crowd, isn't it?" Bold approached, his eyes scanning for Ikota and Romero.

"Yes," Sheila's quiet voice expressed how overwhelmed she felt. She wore a pink blouse and jeans that had a "just bought at the store look." Her dark shoulder length hair hung straight.

"This isn't too bad," Wang dismissed their feelings. "We have many more students in our schools. I'm used to having to push and shove my way into places. America is a piece of cake." He grinned at his use of the idiom.

"The problem I have is that people get offended when I knock them out of the way. But I smile and say, 'excuse me,' and everything's okay. It's all the polite phrases Americans use that get me. I'm sure they don't even mean them." He wore the same jeans and green stripped polo shirt he had worn at the exchange student meeting. Even though he was a few inches taller than Sheila, he looked slight and overwhelmed in the midst of all these American kids.

Bold nodded. Seeing Ikota and Romero enter at the same time but through different doors, Bold raised his arm to wave. "Romero! Ikota! Here!" Several other students turned to look, causing Bold to collapse inward and withdraw his greeting. Fortunately, the two had heard him the first time, so they joined the group anyway.

Ikota's long black hair shimmered in the fluorescent lighting and complimented the silky blue blouse and floral skirt that she wore with grace. Despite the fact that no one else seemed to be as dressed up as she was, there was an inner peace and confidence that Bold admired. This contrasted with Romero's friendly energy. He matched Bold in height, but Romero's hair curled tightly, and his face constantly reflected his appreciation for and enjoyment of whatever life was going on around him. He wore his jeans and white t-shirt with style and drew attention from the other students.

Hi's were shared all around, a deep breath was taken and the five new students entered the foray of their first day of school. They stayed as a group, finding lockers and looking for classrooms. Finally, they knew it was time to separate and face their first classes of the day. They agreed to meet for lunch by the cafeteria door so that they could figure out the lunch system as a team. Just knowing that they would all be back together as a group in the middle of the day, helped ease Bold's growing uneasiness.

Bold and Sheila entered Economics together. Looking away quickly, he couldn't discern if the staring eyes of the other students were friendly, curious or hostile. He assumed the worse as the protective sense of anger began to build inside of him. Being distracted, he stumbled over someone's foot, and the pounding embarrassment was not enough to block out the quiet snickers of a few students sitting nearby. Since the other students were already seated, Bold and Sheila chose two seats next to each other toward the front of the room (the only available seats) and sat, silently encouraging each other in their first real American class. Sheila must have noticed his clumsy entrance, but she said nothing and seemed to desperately need his support to get through this adventure. So, Bold pulled into himself and focused on the task at hand—assimilation.

The Economics teacher was an older man and liked to talk, so Bold settled back and focused on getting used to his style of speech, "discourse style," that's what Todd had called it. Fortunately, it was similar to the tone and patterns of the minister of the Bowers' church, so Bold could understand him more easily than he had expected. Unfortunately, Bold usually tuned Pastor

Reynolds out, and he had to work a little bit at keeping his attention on the teacher's words. When he took a break and glanced around the room, he noticed that many of the students appeared to be as intent on the teacher's introduction as teens in the church were on the pastor's sermon. Bold smirked to himself and allowed his tensed muscles to relax. This might not be too bad.

For second hour he said goodbye to Sheila and headed to room 312, math. He looked forward to this class for two reasons. The first was that math should be easier to understand because it dealt with numbers more than words. Besides, despite the fact that it had not been his favorite class and that he had had to rely on Saraa for help with homework, he had done well with math in Zuunmod, so this should not be too tough. Saraa had always made sure he understood the math and had refused to let him copy her work, which was what students traditionally did. In fact, the teachers encouraged "cheating" in Mongolia, wanting the students to perform well and make them look good with their high marks. But Saraa was different and wanted both Bold and she to learn the material so that they could go on to college and get good jobs.

The second reason he moved a little faster was that both Wang and Ikota would be in math with him. Pre-Calculus might prove to be his safe-haven for the school day. That and Physical Education, which was towards the end of the day.

"Hey, Bold! Come sit by us." Wang's voice welcomed him into Room 312. Ikota's smile drew him across the room without a second thought to any of the other students already occupying the room.

"Hi, how was your first class?" Bold asked them both as he sat down.

"Pretty tough," Ikota admitted first. "The teacher speaks really fast, so I didn't catch everything. It's an advanced Chemistry class and going to be difficult, I think."

"Yeah, I agree," Wang nodded as he spoke. "The syllabus contains a lot of reading and lab work. Maybe once we get going it will become more familiar and feel like classes back home, but we did not do as much lab work in China. I'm used to being told what the right answer is, not figuring it out."

"Well, this class should be better. Numbers are the same in any language." Bold hoped he was right. He really needed something familiar right then.

"That's my seat," the same hulk that had shoved Bold earlier in the day stood over Wang now, demanding that Wang change seats.

"I didn't think the seats were assigned in this class," Wang nervously responded, eyes down and voice carefully modulated.

"They aren't, except for that one. That one's mine."

Just as Wang was collecting his notebooks, the teacher interrupted the one-sided negotiations, "Gentlemen, is there a problem? Mr. Meyer, I believe someone is already sitting in that seat. You may sit in one of the seats over here." She pointed at the remaining seats towards the front of class.

"Okay, Ms. Bruler," casting a backwards glare at Wang, the student took a different seat. Bold eased back into his desk for he had been about to step in.

"Class, come up one at a time and get your textbook. Be sure to write the number of your text next to your name on the sheet." The teacher was a young woman who appeared to be serious about the class and yet also had a sparkle in her eye as if she was capable of having some fun, too.

Sitting down with his book, Bold began scanning the different chapters. The first ones looked familiar, but by the third chapter everything became foreign and complicated looking. Panic surged through his veins, making his heart race as he realized that even this class would be very different from any he had taken in Zuunmod. Swear words exploded in his brain like a firework display, and he carefully kept his head bent to hide the emotions that colored his face.

"Whew! This looks like what we did last year. Maybe I can handle this class," Wang breathed a sigh of relief followed by Ikota's affirmation that she too had a similar text for Pre-Calculus the previous year.

This deepened Bold's shame. He knew he should join the conversation, but he couldn't bring himself to tell his new friends the truth, and faking it just then was impossible. The teacher's handing out of the syllabus saved him from having to do either. At least he would know what was going on for the first couple of weeks. He would just have to work hard and make it look like math was as easy for him as it would be for his two friends.

English with Romero proved challenging but entertaining. Romero seemed to fit into any social situation and did not let his broken English hold him back. Despite Bold's embarrassment for his friend, he appreciated that the spotlight was not on him and that he could laugh with the others over jokes that he actually understood. Romero might not be able to help Bold academically in this class, but he would help him relax and relieve the constant self-consciousness.

Right from the start Romero entered into the class. "First, I would like everyone to introduce him or herself. Tell us your name and something interesting about you." The teacher had begun class. Sinking into his seat, Bold dreaded when it would be his turn, until he realized he could simply say he was from Mongolia and answer the questioning stares of the other students.

"My name Romero, and I love beautiful women." Romero proudly proclaimed.

Some in the back responded, "Was that Romeo? As in 'Romeo, Romeo, wherefore art thou, Romeo'?"

"No, it's Romero, but if the pretty ladies in this class want to call me, 'Romeo,' I happily answer." Everyone laughed, sensing Romero's good-natured confidence. Even the teacher took a moment to regain her composure.

"Where are you from, Romero? Your accent suggests you're not from around here."

"You're right. I came from room 127, down the hall," Romero countered with eyes that danced. "No, really, I come to you from Venezuela. I very pleased to be here to learn all I can about America."

The students clapped their welcome, and the entire atmosphere of the class seemed to relax into one of pleasant acceptance.

"My name is Bold, and I am from Mongolia." Bold forced himself to sit up, speak clearly and face the teacher. He did not want to have to repeat himself.

"Wow, I've never met someone from Mongolia before. It will be fun to learn about it." The teacher commented as Bold heard another student tell his neighbor that "Bold" was a cool name.

The teacher continued to ask questions of various students and made comments, showing that some of them she knew already but that, most of all, she was looking forward to getting to know each of them individually. This enthusiasm for each student stunned Bold and brought back memories of his teachers who focused on the better students and ignored those who could not keep up in a class. Maybe he had a chance even in this one.

"I'm exhausted. Is it time to go home yet?" Wang exhaled as he plopped down at the lunch table with the others. His constant smile belied his weariness. Bold wondered at his energy and ability to adapt so easily.

"What do you mean? The day is just getting started. Consider this a second breakfast." Romero parried, his eyes constantly roving the cafeteria, making contact with others and flashing his winning grin. His networking never seemed to cease. It wore Bold out just to watch him.

"Well, I really do feel tired," Sheila admitted. She did look a little frayed. Bold drew closer to her and stopped himself just before his hand reached out to pat hers as it lay motionless next to her lunch.

"Me, too," Itoka sympathized.

"Oh come on, this place is great. These teachers have so much more personality and energy than my teachers in China." They looked shocked at his change in attitude, but Wang persisted in his pursuit of lifting everyone's spirits as he imitated, speaking his native language, very dry and officious teachers. When he whacked Romero on the head for not answering a question correctly, everyone joined him, at least with real smiles.

"Hey, Mr. Banyon may not have hit us on the head when we missed a question, but he did torture us today with his deadly boring voice," Ikota defended. "Class, you will learn about the history of the world from the beginning of time to the end of time, and your time spent in this class will feel as though you have lived through it all a hundred times over . . ." She droned on, adding details and phrases that the others had heard throughout the day.

"Okay, but what about the lively Miss Spiro?" Romero demanded. Affecting a feminine pose, he continued. "Class, today," he gave his wrist a swing and a twist, "we will spend some time getting to know each other. Won't that be fun?!" He clapped his hands enthusiastically and then tweaked Sheila's cheek. She turned red, and the embarrassment was infused with even more color as she burst out in laughter.

Bold noticed that students at other tables glanced their way, wondering at the noise they were creating. He wanted to return the invasion with a glare but couldn't keep the anger in his eyes as his attention was pulled back into the antics of his own group of friends.

*Friends.* Yes, these were his friends. He needed to stop watching for what others thought of the "outsiders" and start to establish his place among these people who would make the year bearable. With a deep breath and slight shake, Bold did an impromptu imitation of the math teacher, adding in a few hand gestures of his own.

Suddenly, the social temperature dropped. "Speaking of math, I was a bit frightened when that Neanderthal wanted to sit in my desk." Wang's smile dropped from his eyes and turned his smile into a shaky line of consternation.

"I thought he might actually hit you or dump you out of the desk," Ikota agreed, sending soothing empathy with her large, brown eyes.

"I was ready to step in if I had to," Bold's cold rage flashed, clenching his fists involuntarily.

"I'm glad you didn't," Wang smiled waveringly at Bold.

"You probably would have gotten in trouble," Ikota affirmed Wang's response, ignoring the increase in testosterone in the air.

Romero joined, "Yeah, we have to be careful. They maybe come down on us more quick-like because we from other countries. I see bullies here, too. I think friendship is best response. Excuse me, Mr. Bully, but would you hit my left cheek after you hit my right one?" He became a demure victim, mimicking an attack in comic exaggeration.

Instantly, the warmth returned, and camaraderie was restored. Bold took longer to let go of his righteous indignation, but he had to admit to himself that laughter was much more fun than plotting revenge. He flashed to a day in Mongolia when another student had pushed around Saraa's younger brother. Bold had lashed out, first with words and then with fists, guaranteeing that the boy would never bother Baatar again. It had felt good, and then the only consequence had been that the younger boys in school steered clear of Bold after that. What would the consequence of a fight be here in America?

After lunch Bold went to his Physical Education class. Sheila would also be there. He was thankful that Cheryl had insisted on buying him what he would need for the class last week when she picked up things for her own children. He would not have had any idea what to get because they had not changed at his school. He confidently exchanged his school clothes for those in David's old duffle bag and stored everything in a locker.

"Hurry up, people," the teacher blew a whistle and hustled them through a door to the gym where the girls would soon join the class.

Sitting on bleachers the male teacher droned on about expectations and unit topics. Finally, he blew his whistle and told them to grab the basketballs and shoot baskets for the remaining class time. Bold stood next to Sheila and then drew her towards the central hoop.

"Let's join this group," he encouraged her. She shivered in her outfit of shorts and t-shirt. Bold figured it was from both nerves and actual coldness. They rotated through, taking turns to shoot and then retrieve the ball. Bold spoke little but gave Sheila as much positive feedback as he could.

"Hey, are you two a couple?" A tall gangly kid with acne covering his face called out. His sneering tone made it sound dirty and more like a challenge than an honest possibility.

"No," Bold's defensiveness flew out with this one word. When he turned to toss Sheila the ball for her turn, he realized that it had hit and shamed her. "I'm sorry, Sheila, I didn't mean it the way it sounded."

"That's okay. I understand." She let her hair fall to cover her reddening cheeks as she focused on dribbling the ball.

Another boy noticed their discomfort and joined the taunting. "Well, then, how about showing me how you 'do it' where you're from? I hear Asian girls are trained from an early age to please their men." The gangly boy gave him a high five and started gesturing rudely towards Sheila.

Bold stepped between Sheila and the boys. "Where I am from, men treat women with respect," his cheeks burned with indignation at the boys and shame that this statement was not entirely true, "So maybe you should show her some respect."

"We treat everyone with respect in this class, don't we, gentlemen?" The teacher had unobtrusively joined the group, dispersing it immediately.

Later in the locker room, though, the two students walked by Bold as he changed, shoving him with their elbows. "This isn't finished, Asian boy."

# Chapter 7: Cementing Relationships

It took only five weeks for Randy Meyer to set his sights on Bold and his friends. He was the big guy who had bumped into Bold the first day of school. He also had a following, Robby and Marty, the two guys from PE. They admired Randy and laughed at everything he did and said, encouraging him in his demand for attention.

In Calculus, Randy traded off between razzing Wang for participating so much in class discussions to staring at Ikota and making lewd remarks. "Hey, Asian boy, why don't you let the rest of us answer some questions," or "We get it, you're smart, so you can stop showing off now," or "No matter what you think, your country is never going to take over America because we have the real power". This last would be said as he flexed his muscles or waved a fist at Wang. Randy was an artist when it came to bullying and knew when he could get away with it. Either the teacher would be distracted helping another student or talking to someone in the hall, or he would say it just loud enough for only Wang and his friends to hear. Bold wondered why the teacher never noticed how often Randy wandered to their side of the room.

The comments to Ikota really disturbed Bold, though. "How about you and me, tonight, in a hot tub, with only the bubbles between us?" or "You need to lighten up, girl, why not let me show you how American boys treat their women?" The walk-by comments could never be properly addressed, which seemed to relieve Ikota who kept her eyes down and body tightly controlled. Bold would glare at Randy, who would simply wink and smirk at him. One day he leaned in and asked, "Jealous?" before he sauntered back to his desk.

When Bold brought it up at lunch, both Wang and Ikota pleaded with him to let it go. They did not want to draw attention to themselves or get in trouble. The threat of being sent home early loomed over them. Besides, they were used to ignoring such people and not getting involved in violent exchanges.

As for gym class, Robby and Marty left Bold and Sheila alone, except for quiet "pot shots" now and then when the teacher wasn't nearby. They all knew that Bold would win in a fight and that all the two needed was for Bold to throw a punch, and he would be in trouble with the teacher and the school administration. So, Sheila kept Bold's temper from controlling him by letting him know how much she counted on him to be in class with her.

"If it isn't the 'Bold and the Beautiful,'" Randy swaggered up to Bold who was getting his homework for the evening out of his locker. "Are you and that Asian chick, 'I coach ya,' getting it on? She is some piece of work. Will you give me a taste of sushi when you're tired of her?"

Not sure what Randy meant but definite that it was something nasty because of the leer on his face, Bold exploded. He slammed his locker and planted his feet, ready to exchange more than words.

"All right, so you want to fight?!" Randy slowly peeled off his jacket and at the same time lost some of his dominance. Bold was not going to back down, that much was obvious, and Randy's eyes responded with a tinge of fear.

"Hey, what's going on here?" David stepped out of the crowd that had gathered and placed his hand on Bold's tense shoulder. "Randy, don't you need your jacket for going home?" He reached for Randy's jacket as he moved to place himself between the two combatants.

"I will, but first I have to finish something." Randy's forced vibrato told Bold that he could win this fight but that it would be a hollow victory. Randy had not expected a fight. He had expected Bold to back down like most people did when he harassed them. Maybe he should just finish things right here and now.

But then David continued, "Come on, guys. Neither of you wants trouble with the office. You'll be suspended for sure. You've been in enough trouble, Randy, and this might be the final straw. Besides, if you force the issue, I'll just have to stand alongside my brother here. Do you think you can take both of us on?" David stepped back next to Bold.

"Both of you? That's not fair! You are such wusses!" Randy grabbed his coat and stalked off, not allowing anyone to say or do anything else.

Bold knew that Randy had not really wanted to fight and that David had given him a way to save face. He thanked David with a slight nod and eye-connection. Inside a sense of well-being drowned out the rage as he heard the words, "My brother," played over and over through his mind. Both boys walked to the bus, sitting next to each other and discussing their homework for that night.

Just before the bus reached their stop, "Bold, the youth group at church is having an evangelism celebration tonight; do you want to come?" David had stopped inviting Bold to youth group meetings since school began because Bold always had so much homework and used that as an excuse to avoid the uncomfortable social situation of not only being surrounded by strangers but being surrounded by strangers who talked about the spiritual world and a God they really believe existed. It seemed creepy to Bold and a little insane.

But the connectedness from earlier that day felt so good that Bold did not want to break it just yet. "Sure, it sounds fun." Apprehension washed over Bold as the implication of his words hit him, but the pure pleasure in David's eyes at his acceptance dried him off quickly.

"Great. We leave at 6:15 to get there early and get seats."

"Okay." Both collected their gear and disembarked to home and to their separate rooms for homework.

"Welcome, everyone, to our 'Evangelism Celebration'! Tonight we have music, drama, games and a challenge that should make you all think seriously about what the real purpose of life is." Bold sat forward as the youth pastor, Toby, began the meeting.

Toby wore worn jeans that Bold would have worn to milk horses in or to prepare the meal for a horhog (Mongolian barbecue), but he would never have worn such an outfit to speak to a large group in a church. Yet, the jeans seemed appropriate for the open and accepting way Toby reached to everyone around him. As he spoke, Toby made eye contact with each person, speaking as if it he was having a private conversation with a friend. Bold especially felt this way when Toby prayed before the singing. Either Toby was completely deluded, or he was speaking to a God whom he knew on a personal level. But how could that possibly be?

The prayers he had heard in the Buddhist temple were almost sung and came from written texts. There was nothing personal or informal about them. Was Toby being disrespectful? Bold wasn't sure, but his curiosity had been ignited.

Many of the songs were unfamiliar to Bold, and he felt on the outside of things as everyone around him sang with abandon and sincerity. Bold did enjoy singing the traditional Mongolian songs about their country and about mothers; everyone would join in, even during concerts. But he could not join in as the teens around him sang about a God Bold still doubted truly existed, or at least who did not exist for Bold. This was America's God, not Mongolia's. Yet the people here did not seem to make that distinction.

After energetic singing, confusing and disturbing skits (especially the one about a young girl who wanted to go with her friends to Heaven but was not allowed in because she did not know Jesus) and some ridiculously hilarious games, everyone settled down with red faces and sweaty foreheads to listen to Toby. "Tonight, I want you to think about the purpose of your life. What is driving your choices? Where are you headed? Why do you do and say the things that you do and say?

"Many of you here tonight claim to be Christians, claim to be Christ's followers, but what does that really mean? Where is He leading you? Do you know?

"In Ephesians 6, Paul writes, 'We are His workmanship, created in Christ Jesus for good works, which He has prepared beforehand for us.' God created you to be unique and special. He created you to make a difference in the world through good works that you are to accomplish. These good works have already been established. Are you doing them?

"Or are you living your life for yourself? Are you moving from one 'fun' experience to the next, marking off time in this world, and making the best of it for yourself? Maybe you are racing after fulfillment as the World defines fulfillment—in relationships, material things, competition, winning, achieving, and so on. What defines you? What makes you feel the most satisfied and accomplished? Is it doing God's will? Is it completing the Kingdom work He has assigned for you to do? How do we even know what the work is that we have been created for?"

Bold noticed several of the teens shift in their seats. They were taking Toby's words to heart. They believed this stuff about a Living God who had an individual purpose for each person. Amazing!

"Well, the first step is to make sure you are a member of God's family, a citizen of His Heavenly Kingdom. To do that you simply must believe that Jesus came as a man, lived among us, died on the cross, an innocent man, to pay for the sin and evil that separates us from God, and then arose from the dead, extending that same victory of death, that same miraculous life, to us. God wants you to enter into a personal, authentic relationship with Himself. Are you ready? Have you made that step yet?"

A cloud of confused defenses distracted Bold from hearing Toby's remarks to those who already believe in Jesus. He worked on keeping his eyes pointed at Toby, but nothing else was allowed to penetrate.

Fortunately, Bold rarely spoke around the Bowers, so David and Michael did not pester him with questions or wonder at his withdrawal as they headed home. Discussions Bold had had with his family and friends battled with comments and ideas he had begun to discover here in America through the Bowers and his friends at school. What was his purpose in life? What would it mean if he accepted this American God?

That night Bold slept little and awoke with the determination that he just did not know what to believe and that he would not be able to decide while here. He would have to wait until he returned home. Right now he was taking in all that he could, but he had to be careful that he did not change so much that he did not fit into his old life.

"Bold, are you up?" It was Saturday, a day Bold usually enjoyed starting around 11:00.

"Sure, Cammy." He rolled over reluctantly but sat up with interest when he saw the urgency in her blue eyes.

"I need some advice, and everyone else is gone or too busy."

"What is it?" He moved over, making room for her on the edge of the bed.

As she sat next to him, Cammy explained her dilemma. "There's this girl at school who picks on me. She calls me a 'fanatic' and asks me what God says to me when I pray. I don't mind the teasing, but yesterday she pushed me so hard at recess that I fell down and scraped my knee. She said that she was going to be beat me up after school next week, and then we would see if my God was real. She said that if He really loved me He would take care of me and protect me from her."

Tears welled up as she confessed her fears and admitted her doubts about what she should do. She did not want to get beat up, but, more importantly, she did not want Samantha, the bully, to think that God did not exist. Her desire to protect God's reputation warmed Bold's heart, but Samantha's audacity and cruelty scalded it. He wanted to teach Samantha the same lesson he had taught back in Mongolia.

Yet, that had not been the solution that David had gone for when faced with Randy Meyers. Besides, Bold did not go to the same school as Cammy, so he could not easily just step in and protect her. He could not even offer to stand next to her as David had stood next to him. This was not going to be an easy problem to solve.

The issues were so much bigger here. God's reality was at stake. Bold had to admit that he sided with Samantha in her assertion that God would not take care of Cammy. Momentarily, it bothered him that Cammy was being forced to defend this supposedly all-superior God who ruled all things. If He was real, why would he allow Cammy to be in such a situation? But then again, what could He do for Cammy besides comfort her while she recovered from her injuries? According to Toby, Jesus had taken a beating for things He had not done. Is this what it meant to be a Christian?

Cammy sat silently next to Bold, relaxed now that she had shared her dilemma. The fact that Bold said nothing beyond, "This is a difficult situation," did not seem to faze her. She leaned back on his shoulder, expressing confidence that he would eventually figure out what she should do.

The silence unsettled Bold more than Cammy, so he felt compelled to interrupt it with the best deflection he could devise. "Cammy, maybe I should think about this. I will tell you my idea later today. Okay?"

"Okay," and with complete confidence she bounded out of his room to play.

Bold sank back into his bed, realizing that the advice he gave must reflect the beliefs and values of the Bowers, not his own. What would Cheryl or Matt tell Cammy to do? David would be much better at giving appropriate advice, but he and Michael were gone for the weekend on a leadership retreat for the youth group. About ready to give up, Bold realized that Ikota and Romero both talked about their Christian faith, sounding a lot like the Bowers. They should be able to tell Bold what he can tell Cammy.

Skipping a shower, Bold dressed and commandeered the upstairs hallway phone, hoping to get through to Ikota or Romero before Cammy came back for an answer. But both friends were out for the day. Bold had to figure this out for himself. The fact that Cammy had come to him and trusted him to help her made him want to come through for her. Maybe the best thing would be to just confide in Cheryl whom he could hear in the kitchen below. A weight lifted as he turned towards the stairs to descend.

"Bold, I have to run some errands. Will you look after Cammy for a few hours?" Most likely reading the disappointment in his face, she added, "Do you have any other plans? I can take her with me if you do." Cheryl's voice forced the weight of Cammy's problem back onto Bold's shoulders.

"Sure, no problem," he replied, trying to assert confidence. "I have much homework to do today."

"Thank you!" He heard the door close with finality. This was up to him and him alone. Or was it? Bold had heard people pray plenty while in America. Isn't that what Cammy should do now? The Bowers prayed about everything from problems at Matt's work to health needs. They believed that God was real and involved in their lives. Shouldn't Cammy put the problem back on God's shoulders instead of coming to Bold who knew so little about how Americans handle conflicts? He realized she was young and did not understand the cultural differences, but Bold was reminded every day that he was in a foreign land among foreign people.

"Cammy!" He called out before he changed his mind.

"Yeah?!" She immediately appeared; her face filled with hopeful expectation. "Have you come up with a solution?"

"Sort of," Bold floundered for words and bought time by leading her down the stairs into the den where they could sit together on the sofa.

"What do you usually do when you have difficulties that you can't handle by yourself?" he asked as they settled into the rose colored cushions.

"I pray." She immediately responded. "And I have prayed about this. I have prayed and prayed, ever since she threatened me. But I still don't know what to do. My Sunday school teacher, Mrs. Ryberg says that we should seek advice from those older than us when we don't get an answer to our prayers." She confidently turned the problem back over to Bold.

"Didn't the pastor say that we should look to the Bible for answers? What did people in the Bible do when they were faced with such mean enemies? Did they fight back, or did they avoid the fight by hiding?" Bold asked the questions, hoping Cammy would know the answers because he did not. In fact, he was curious to know what the Bible had to say about bullies and threats of this nature. The school year was not over yet, and he might have to face Randy once again. He hated to respond in a way that would make the Bower's ashamed of him. He had started to desire their approval more and more as he watched the way they supported and encouraged their own children.

"Let me see. David faced up to the giant Goliath with a slingshot and five stones. He knocked Goliath dead with one shot. Goliath is kind of like Samantha because he talked bad about God, too. But I think God loves Samantha and wants her to believe in Him. I don't think that killing her with a rock to the forehead would help her get to Heaven." The twinkle in her eye told Bold that Cammy was not seriously considering meeting Samantha's threat with an attack of her own.

"I can see you now. 'Hey, Samantha, you'd better stop making fun of God or He will strike you dead!' Then a lightning bolt comes from the sky, a clear sky, and knocks Samantha off her feet." The laughter relaxed both of them and helped them to honestly think about the problem.

"Jesus told people to 'turn the other cheek.'"

"What does that mean?" Bold no longer felt embarrassed about admitting when he did not understand things. The Bowers had proven over and over that they would not look down on him or consider him stupid for not knowing something.

"It means that we should not get revenge when someone hurts us, but we should open up to them and let them hurt us again."

"Why?"

"Because we are to show people the love of God by forgiving others just as God forgives us for the many times we hurt Him."

"How do we hurt God?"

"We hurt Him when we do bad things, when we disobey His laws, like 'do not lie,' 'do not steal,' 'do not murder' and 'worship only God.' When we hurt someone else that God has created, which is everyone, then we hurt God because He loves us so much. He really cares about what happens to us." Cammy sat back, reflecting on the Truths she had just spoken. Bold waited for her, storing away this wisdom for later consideration.

Suddenly, with an inner brightness shining through, Cammy sat forward, grabbing Bold's hand into her own. "You're right, Bold. God wouldn't want me to fight Samantha, which is a good thing because I can't fight. He wants me to pray for her and to love her. I've been praying for myself and asking God to take Samantha out of my life. He wants me to bring her into my life, though. I think I'll call and ask if she wants to go with me to church tomorrow." Without waiting for a response, Samantha raced for the phone. Problem solved.

Bold exhaled as he plunged back into the cushions. What a day! Maybe he should just go back to bed and start it all over again. Before he could get up, however, Cammy bounced back into the den.

"Thank you, Bold!" She threw her arms around Bold's neck. "You are the best!"

Cammy left the room filled with sunshine and a smile of satisfaction on Bold's face. The redness in his cheeks was not from anger this time.

# Chapter 8: What's in a Relationship?

"Hi, Bold," Ruthie once again fell into step with Bold as he walked from 5th to 6th periods. Her grey eyes framed by stylish brown hair invited Bold to consider more than just an acquaintance.

"Hi, Ruthie, how are you?" Bold's discomfort escalated as it always did when she elicited conversation from him. The pressure of her quiet, smiling glances made the four- minute passing time seem an hour.

"Fine. Has anyone asked you to the Sadie Hawkins' Dance, Bold?"

"No." He had no idea where this conversation was going.

"Would you go with me?"

This petition communicated such vulnerability that it produced an immediate response of acquiescence. His cultural instincts answered for him, "Sure, Ruthie. What happens at this dance?"

With dancing eyes and unburied enthusiasm, Ruthie explained the "rules of the engagement." "We'll wear matching shirts. I know you don't drive, so I'll pick you up at 6:00. We'll go out for dinner; don't worry I'll pick somewhere to go. But you do have to pay for dinner. I'll buy the tickets for the dance. That starts at 7:30, so we'll go there from dinner. We'll dance, have our pictures taken, and afterwards I'll take you home. Then on Saturday I'll pick you up for a picnic lunch that I'll pack myself. There will be about us 12 of us total, so it should be a lot of fun."

"12 of us?" Bold's head was spinning.

"Yeah, the two of us, my five best friends and their dates. It'll be a blast." The dreamy look in her eyes revealed that she had already planned and lived out their weekend in a romantic euphoria.

Only then did Saraa's face push its way into Bold's mind. What had he done? What should he do now? This date meant more to Ruthie than it could ever mean to him. Maybe he would simply not be home when she came Friday night to pick him up. That is what he would do in Mongolia, and she would accept his absence.

"See ya tomorrow, Bold," Ruthie moved triumphantly away. Bold responded to her victory walk with interest and wondered if going to the dance could be seen as 'just another cultural experience.'

"Bold to earth," Wang snapped his fingers in front of Bold who now sat in a seat that he didn't remember reaching.

"Hey, man, you okay?" Romero plopped down in the seat next to him, sounding concerned.

"I'm fine. Ruthie just asked me to the Sadie Hawkins' Dance."

"Great! Are you going?" Wang asked enviously.

"I think so. At least I said, 'yes'."

"Super! Suzy asked me. Maybe we can double date." Romero leaned towards him happily.

"I don't think so. She said something about 12 of us going together. Then there's a picnic on Saturday."

"She must really like you, man." Romero spoke with confidence and worldly wisdom.

"I guess so," Bold's short, apathetic answers alerted his two friends.

"So, what's wrong then, Bold?" Wang leaned on his desk, pulling Bold's mind into the conversation by his direct stare.

"I have a girlfriend in Mongolia."

"Oh right, Saraa. Do you think that going on the date with Ruthie will be a betrayal to Saraa?" Wang asked with no indication of a right or wrong answer.

"Of course it would be." Romero assuredly responded, drawing unsure looks from both Wang and Bold.

"But she's not here; she would never know." Wang challenged, sensing that Bold was powerless to respond.

"She is if she is in Bold's heart."

"But I didn't ask Ruthie to go to the dance. How could I say, 'no'? I will just go and have some fun. It seems that most of what I do is study. I would like to see what a dance is like here." Bold's defiance grew with his words, as did his determination to go to the dance with Ruthie.

"What about Ruthie? She doesn't know about Saraa, does she? What if she really likes you? You play with her heart, and no one wins." Romero spoke with authority and almost convinced Bold to immediately leave and tell Ruthie he couldn't go. But then class started, and the dance was forgotten.

In fact, he did not think about it until the bus ride home when David mentioned that he had been asked by Louise Smith.

"Are you going?" Bold asked, assuming the answer would be yes. Louise was in his English class, and he could tell that the other boys really admired her. She was pretty and wore clothes that revealed many of her womanly traits. He thought she looked sad and desperate for attention, but he tried not to judge others in a culture he did not understand.

"No, I told her that I couldn't accept her invitation. It was so hard. She looked so hurt at first. But then she pulled herself together and looked at me with total loathing. 'It was going to be a pity date anyway, David,' she spit out at me as she walked away."

"I'm sorry," Bold did not know why he felt the need to apologize to David, but he did, and David's responding gaze told him it had been the right thing to say.

"I suppose she'll be talking me down now for a while, but she'll get tired of that soon enough. I really don't know why she asked me, and maybe I should have accepted just to be a Christian witness, but everyone knows what she is like and what people expect to happen on a date with her."

"Is what 'everyone knows' true?" Bold asked with sincere curiosity.

David jerked as if he had been slapped. "Bold, you're right. I treated her like everyone else really. Except, instead of eagerly wanting what I thought she was offering, I rejected her for what I assumed she was offering. Jesus would never have turned someone away because He thought they were not morally good enough for Him. None of us is morally good enough for Him, and yet He pursues us and desires to know us and to be known by us more than anything. I think I blew it, Bold. I think I'll stop by church and talk to Toby about how I should make it right."

Bold could not understand David's reasoning, but he felt empathy for David's confusion and regret. Without really thinking about it he asked, "Can I come, too? I was asked as well and think maybe I did not respond in the right way."

"Sure, Bold. We'll ask mom if we can go as soon as we get home. The sooner I get this taken care of, the better I'll feel."

"Me, too." Bold liked this sense of common dilemma and shared hope.

Later Bold found himself sitting with David and Toby in the church's fellowship hall. It had comfortable chairs for talking through tough situations. He sat back and let David talk about his faux pas first. Toby listened as David quickly got to the heart of the matter. "So, I don't think I should take Louise to the dance because I am not interested in dating her, but she took a risk asking me, and I rejected her. I was honest, but my honesty was blunt and hurtful. It was also filled with judgment."

David's shame burned in his face.

"Let's pray first," Toby said, lowering his head. "Father God, please join us here and guide us. We need your wisdom and ask that you show us the right thing to do. We love you and thank you for caring about us so much that even this incident is important to you." A silent pause allowed each of them to accept God's presence in the discussion.

"Okay, I agree that dating a girl whom you don't know well is not healthy. You want to take your time and look for a young woman who shares your passion for Christ. But despising Louise is just like killing her."

Bold sat forward, startled at this statement.

"I know. You talked about it when we went through the Sermon on the Mount," David agreed. "To view someone with contempt is to say in our hearts that that person does not deserve to live in the same world as we do. That is exactly how I looked at Louise." David dropped his head into his hands, and Toby laid his hand on his shoulder.

"You're right, David. Now, what is the solution?" Toby's gentleness held no condemnation, and Bold had hope that things might be made right.

"Dear Lord, please forgive me for judging Louise and for looking down on her as if she was not worthy. None of us are, especially me right now with this sin in my heart. Thank you for providing forgiveness and cleanness through the blood of Jesus. I ask for and accept that forgiveness now. Help me to make it right with Louise, Lord. Give me the words to say, and the opportunity to say them. Thank you. Amen."

"Amen." Toby echoed, then hugged David to himself as the young man wept.

Bold could not tell if David was sad or happy. He sat silently back and watched the older man comfort the younger, realizing that he had never seen two men interact with such gentleness and emotion, other than drunks, that is.

"That's good, David. What will you say to her?"

"I will apologize and explain that she deserves a date with someone who knows her better and likes her just for who she is. It won't be easy because I don't want to put her down in the process."

"Be careful. The apology should set the tone and allow her to hear what you have to say. Why don't you invite her to the next Outreach Celebration?"

"That's a great idea." David's voice and face expressed peace and joy in such a pure form.

"Now, what about you, Bold?" Toby and David both turned their attention towards him.

"Ruthie asked me to the dance. I accepted, but I have a girlfriend back in Mongolia. Can I go, just to see what an American dance is like?" Bold hoped that they would reinforce this solution, the easiest one to follow through on.

"Does Ruthie know that you only consider her a friend and that you have a girlfriend in Mongolia?" Toby asked, dashing Bold's hopes for an easy solution.

"No."

"Does she really like you?" David asked.

"I think so. She didn't say so, but she has everything planned. We're even going on a picnic Saturday." Bold's heart sank lower as he recognized his betrayal of Saraa. He struggled to revive his rationale, "But doesn't it matter that I have never 'led her on'?" He remembered the phrase from Todd's class.

"You can never tell what is going on in a girl's mind, Bold, and your yes would definitely have given her reason to hope that you liked her back. How would you feel if you returned to Mongolia and discovered that Saraa had gone to the school dance with someone? Would you be happy that she had gone out and had a good time, or would you wonder about her feelings for you?" Toby's question penetrated to the core of Bold's uncertainty.

"I would be angry," Bold spoke without censoring and with great vehemence. "I would want to know who it was and would maybe tell Saraa to go be his girlfriend." As if it had really happened, the hurt and rage surged up in his heart. Bold realized the feelings were all too familiar and common. Looking into the startled eyes of Toby and David, he saw the violence that had become a part of him.

"Then I think you have your answer, Bold. The question is how you are going to handle it with Ruthie. I doubt she would like to change her dreams and go 'just as friends.' She'd be humiliated in front of her friends and might try to seduce you throughout the weekend. In her mind it would always be a 'date,' even if you establish that it isn't. On the other hand, you have said yes, and she is counting on you. You will hurt her deeply when you say no, especially after she has told her friends that she is going with you."

"Will it help if I tell her about Saraa? Maybe I can explain that I would like to go, but I did not understand what it would mean in her culture for me to accept. In Mongolia everyone says yes and then decides later if they plan to do something or not. Would she understand these things?" Bold looked pleadingly at Toby.

"I think honesty is the best way to do it. Relationships are so important, Bold. You must always protect those who are most important to you. Tell us about Saraa."

Bold exhaled and sat back as he pictured Saraa. "She is strong and beautiful and full of life. She does not have an easy life and works hard to take care of her family, but she still gets good grades. She is the smartest person I know, and yet she can be silly and talk to little kids so that they understand her."

"She sounds wonderful. Every day that you do what is right and keep your heart pure for her, you honor her, Bold. You show the world that she is worthy of the best, the best that is in you, the best that you can be."

Suddenly Bold understood the real meaning of love. It was about the other person and about bringing out what's good and beautiful in each other. That is what he and Saraa did when they were together. That is what Matt and Cheryl did for each other.

"God also loves you, Bold, and desires the best in you to come out. He wants you to realize how great and grand He is and that He desires your entire heart, your loyalty. Satan, God's enemy, makes other tempting offers, just like Ruthie seemed to offer you a fun weekend, experiencing 'American culture,' but in the end there is always a cost. When you betray your true love, then you lose trust and communicate that the relationship isn't really that important to you. The potential depth and intensity of the relationship has been compromised."

So many words. Bold began to lose track, but he heard that Toby viewed a relationship with God to be of the same nature as a man's relationship with a woman. A commitment had to be made and maintained. It sounded threatening and too intense for Bold. But he would take Toby's advice about Ruthie. It would be hard, but he wanted to do the right thing. He did not want to hurt Ruthie or Saraa, especially Saraa.

"Thank you," Bold shook Toby's hand and quickly exited, knowing David would take longer to say good-bye. He wanted time to think and plan his conversation with Ruthie.

"Hi, Bold," Ruthie grabbed his arm, establishing proprietorship. "Would you like blue, green or red shirts?"

Bold cleared his throat and stopped, pulling Ruthie out of the general traffic flow. "Ruthie, I must talk to you. I made a very big mistake and did not know what I was doing. I am sorry."

"What are you talking about? Is something wrong, Bold?" The confusion on her face compelled Bold to force more words of explanation out.

"I have a girlfriend in Mongolia. Her name is Saraa. She is beautiful and makes me laugh. We have known each other our whole lives and plan to marry some day. I am sorry."

"But she is in Mongolia, Bold. What does that have to do with the dance this weekend? That is what this is leading up to, isn't it?" She pulled back from him; her face crumpled in pain.

"Yes, it means that I should not go to the dance with you and your friends. I think you are a nice girl. You are pretty and smart and fun to talk to. I would like to be your friend, but I do not want to hurt you by going to a dance with you when you like me more than I can allow myself to like you. It would not be right to treat Saraa this way, either."

"She does not have to know," Ruthie said hopefully.

"She would because I would know. I must keep trust with her. I am sorry. I did not mean to hurt you, Ruthie." Bold's burning face drew pity out of Ruthie's heart. She wanted to slap him, to scream at him, to beg him to reconsider, to cry out in pain, but she could not deny the sincere remorse that Bold felt. Bold watched the emotions flash in her eyes and then sighed with relief when the final verdict was acceptance.

"Okay. I really do like you, Bold, but I admire that you want to be faithful to Saraa. She is very lucky. I suppose I'd like you less if you did go to the dance with me. Do you mind if I tell my friends about Saraa? It will make it easier."

"Sure. Tell them anything to help you save face."

"Thanks. I think the truth will be best."

"Do you go to church?" Bold asked, suddenly recognizing an integrity in Ruthie that mirrored the acceptance and forgiveness he had often seen (and sometimes experienced) in the Bowers, Romero and Ikota.

"Yes, I do. Do you?" She smiled openly.

"Yes, with the Bowers. You are a good person, Ruthie."

"Thank you. So are you, Bold." She turned and left, not beaten but not so triumphant, either.

# Chapter 9: Release

"Hey, Bold, what are you doing this weekend?" Sheila asked as he sat down next to her in first hour.

"Studying." Canceling his date the previous week with Ruthie had reinforced how much he missed his friends and his social life in Mongolia.

"Would you like to come to my host family's house for a small party Friday night? They said I could have a few people over." Sheila blushed.

"Sure, have you asked anyone else?" Bold hoped Ikota, Wang and Romero would be there, too. He would love to have more time to get to know these people who always gave snippets of interesting views on the topics that came up at lunch, in classes or when they met to study after school in the library.

"Not yet, but I plan to. If you want to mention it to Wang and Ikota next hour in math, that would be fine. I think it's time to relax and have some fun." Bold realized that he had only been thinking of his own loneliness. Most likely all of them were feeling on the outer edge of life here.

"Yes, I agree."

Class began, ending the need to talk.

Bold almost forgot about the party at Sheila's. Just as he exited Calculus with Wang and Ikota he remembered. "Sheila said to invite you both to her host family's house on Friday for a small party. I hope you can go."

"It sounds like fun. I'll have to check first, but I don't have any other plans." Ikota infused irony into her response.

"Count me in," Wang enthused. "I could use a party. I wonder what they are like in America."

"I don't know, but ours will probably be different. It will probably be like no party in any country." Ikota laughed and moved off to her next class.

At lunch they discussed plans, and all agreed that they must ask their surrogate parents first for the final say. "I hope everyone can come," Sheila voiced what everyone else felt.

Bold waited for Cheryl as she gave last minute instructions to Michael who would be taking care of Cammy Friday night. David and his dad had already gone to dinner and then would go to the batting cages for some practice and father/son time. Cheryl was going to meet with some friends to "scrap book," the latest fad for busy mothers according to Matt.

"Here is Sheila's house, Bold. I'll wait until you get inside before I leave, so if there's a problem or you need something, just come out and tell me." Cheryl routinely thought of the needs of her family before setting out to do her own thing Bold noticed.

"Thank you. Bye." He lugged a bag of groceries that Cheryl had helped him buy. Each of them was to bring ingredients for a favorite meal from his/her country. Bold looked forward to eating buuz and trying the foods that the others would make. It had been much too long.

"Hey, Bold!" Sheila had the door open before he even reached the steps. "Everyone else is here. It looks like you've come prepared." Her welcoming smile shone with anticipation, reminding Bold that he wasn't the only one looking forward to tonight.

As he stepped into the door, Romero greeted him and took his bag of groceries. Bold noticed the neat line of shoes in the front hall and added his own. The creamy carpet must be protected from any dirt, he assumed, as he noticed that the room immediately to the right of the entryway was immaculately kept. There were no nicks in the furniture, sparking crystal vases and candy dishes sat elegantly on display, pristine pictures of nowhere special hung straight and regal on the unmarked cream walls. Did a family really live here? This didn't seem to match the noisy family Sheila often described.

Sheila explained quickly, "This is the front room and never used. I don't think anyone goes in there except to clean it. Maybe if an important guest came, that person would be invited in, but so far that hasn't happened while I've been here."

She shrugged and led him into a kitchen which gleamed with a "just cleaned" freshness but did look much more utilitarian than "the front room"; people definitely used this kitchen. They would have to clean up after themselves, and then some, in this place. Bold thought about the differences in the rooms and realized that many Mongolians did the same thing—presented a beautiful front that hid the ugly truths of their real lives. No wonder so many people felt misunderstood and alone.

He then thought of the lived in comfort of the Bowers' home, which was often clean but never "picture perfect." They never minded if people dropped by or if someone brought a friend home. People just had to take the lived-in "mess" for what it was. Life and people were much more important than impressions. Bold would sometimes be embarrassed when David had friends over or Cheryl's women friends stopped by for a "chat and cup of coffee" as he noticed covered tables, dirty dishes and unfinished projects cluttering the various rooms. No one else seemed to mind, though. Then they would all pull together to clean the house and put everything back into its place.

He remembered the mess that Michael and David had made the Saturday they made breakfast for the rest of the family. Pancake batter had spattered everywhere, including the light fixture hanging from the ceiling. Cheryl had noticed but had expressed nothing but appreciation for the work the boys had done. She did make them clean up after, but Bold had walked in on her cleaning up their 'clean up' an hour later. "You caught me, Bold. Please don't tell the boys. I don't want them to think they shouldn't ever be in the kitchen." She had winked at him and gone back to work on the light fixture.

Ikota poked her tiny nose into Bold's bag, "What are you going to make, Bold?"

"Buuz," he replied. "They are meat dumplings. Usually we use mutton, but I could only find ground beef. They won't be as good as ours in Mongolia, but you will get the idea. My mom makes the very best."

"Sounds good," Romero patted his stomach. Sheila rolled her eyes.

"Hey, Romero, how did the dance go? You never said anything about it last week," Wang asked as they continued unpacking their various ingredients for the evening's meal.

"It was mistake. I should follow Bold's example and not gone. Suzy was much more interested in me than me in her. In fact, she grabbed at me and tried to kiss me throughout the long night. I was embarrassed for her and me." For the first time since meeting him, Bold saw Romero's golden brown cheeks flared up.

"I'm sorry," Ikota patted his arm gently.

"Thanks, me too," Romero shrugged and then forced his face back into its usual gleaming smile, "But we live and learn, no? Let's cook! You will all love the pasta dish I am about to create."

"How should we do this? Should we just cook at the same time, or should we have one person make a dish and teach the others while it's being made?" Sheila quickly took control of the group. She didn't seem nervous at all, not having stuck her raven black hair behind her ears once.

"I'd like to see how people make their food. Maybe we can begin with something that will be cooking for a long time and do various parts of each dish to try and finish them all up at the same time." Ikota proposed.

"Sounds like a plan," Wang nodded at Ikota.

The group of friends busily got to work, turning the conversation to the foods they were making, when they would eat these dishes in their home countries and what ingredients had been substituted. Sheila kept them on track and saw to it that they cleaned up as they went along. Bold appreciated her organization and soft-spoken commands.

Saraa would have been similar; however, her directions would have been more to the point. Mongolians did not use as many polite phrases as Americans did, nor did they raise their voices as much as Americans; some of the students at school seemed to scream everything they said. The noise alone wore him out at the end of the school day. He suspected that Koreans were more polite, like Americans, because Sheila never seemed to forget to include a please or thank you with her requests.

Biting into his buuz, Bold waited for the infusion of greasy broth. His heart sank when very little spilled out of the dumpling into his homesick mouth. The hamburger had been too lean and just did not taste like the fatty mutton used back home. No matter how much he learned and how much he adapted to the routines of American life, the food never satisfied him like the traditional food of Mongolia. At least he could count on a big celebration when he returned home and would be able to eat his fill of buuz, aaral (hardened cheese curds), airak (fermented mare's milk), huushur (fried dumplings) and milk tea.

"Hey, Bold, these are good," Romero broke into Bold's reverie as he polished off his first buuz.

"Thanks, it's not as good as my mom makes, but it will do." Bold realized that these counterfeit buuz probably tasted closer to foods the others were used to than the real (jinkin) buuz he ate at home.

Cheryl had asked him to make buuz for them sometime, too, and these would be a hit with the Bowers. They would think that eating Mongolian food was not really that different from the variety of other foods they ate. Oh well, maybe someday they would visit him in his homeland, and then they would taste his life for real. Or would that be shameful? Would they look down on him for the small apartment and his limited wardrobe? Would the food make them sick? Would they pity him after seeing the reality of his life there?

"Bold to earth," Wang snapped his fingers in his left ear. "You sure do disappear sometimes, Bold."

"Sorry," Bold met their eyes and realized that he needed to return from Mongolia and be with his friends in America. "I was thinking about home."

"Yeah, eating food from Japan has made me nostalgic, too," Ikota nodded towards Bold with understanding.

"To our home countries," Romero raised his glass of apple juice. Everyone did the same and offered salutations in their own languages.

"Do you ever wonder what it will be like to return?" Sheila asked. "I mean, I know that I've changed, and people at home won't have. How will they respond to the new me? I'm not sure I want to go back to being the old me, either."

"I don't think I've changed much. What kind of changes are you talking about, Sheila? Is it the clothes you wear now? I've noticed that you dress more casually than you did at first. You still seem to be pretty quiet and polite." Wang's sincerity elicited a further response from Sheila who colored deeply.

"Well, do you remember when Bold told me about the Buddhist temple on the edge of town? Ikota went with me and then invited me to the church where she attends. The two were so different. At the temple it seemed ghostly and as if the gods were far away and unmoved by the constantly repeated petitions of the people.

"It did feel like the temple at home, and at first I enjoyed the familiarity, but the Christian church was so different. People greeted each other and took time to listen to how others were really doing. One woman shared with her friend that her husband had just lost his job. The woman pulled out her billfold and handed her friend money to help with bills. The prayers were like real conversations, honoring and petitioning a God who listened and was involved in their lives.

"I felt welcomed and loved immediately. I have never felt that way as a Buddhist. The message asserted that I mattered and that God wanted me to be part of His Kingdom. I wanted to belong so much that I kept going back with Ikota."

Bold had noticed that Ikota and Sheila seemed to share a special friendship but had assumed that it was just because they were girls. Girls always seemed to develop deeper relationships than guys. At least Saraa entered relationships with her heart ready and fought to understand and help others much more than he could ever motivate himself to do. He just never seemed able to care that much about the lives and problems of others.

Suddenly, Bold realized this was not true, though. He had come to care much more deeply about the Bowers and their concerns than he had thought he ever could. It must be because they cared so openly for him.

"Anyway, I'm a Christian now, and I know there are many good churches in Korea, but what will my family say? Will they let me make my own choice in this matter? Or will they think I am turning my back on them? Korean girls are brought up to obey and please their parents. I do not want to dishonor my parents by practicing a different religion from them."

Seeming to miss the real dilemma, Romero stood and walked over to hug Sheila, "Welcome to the family, Sheila. We're brother and sister now, you know. Christians are one big family."

Her face glowed with joy, erasing the worry lines that had just creased it, "Thank you, *brother* Romero. I am very happy."

Wang interrupted the "reunion," expressing his discomfort, "Hey, wait a minute. Sheila, are you sure you've really thought about this? Maybe when you get home to your Buddhist friends and family, you'll realize that this was just another American experience for you. You might not have any real problem going back to your old habits and beliefs once the unfamiliarity of America is gone. I'd be quiet about my new beliefs when I first got home and make sure they were real. It might just be a coping strategy you've developed here and won't need back home."

Bold listened with some agreement but anxiously turned to Sheila to hear her response. How real was this change for her?

"No, I don't think I'll ever want to return to my old beliefs. This is real, Wang. God is real. I have never felt so alive or so happy in my life. The Creator of the Universe cares about me and has chosen me to interact with in a special relationship. I can't give Him up now that I've finally found Him."

"He sounds like your lover or something," Wang joked.

"He is," Sheila blushed furiously and dropped her eyes, indicating that she could not speak anymore on the topic.

"I know it's hard to understand that someone could have a relationship with One whom others cannot see or hear, but Christians do hear God's voice and do see His work throughout their days, Wang. God is very real and can be experienced through our spirits." Ikota spoke up to distract the attention from Sheila and to further explain things to Wang.

"I don't have a spirit." Wang defied her inference that he was missing out on something very special and could simply choose to experience it for himself. Bold noticed that his eyes shifted and were filled with more uncertainty and less bravado than his voice suggested.

"Well, Wang, if you ever want to know more about this God, just ask any of us," Romero swept his hand to include himself and the two girls. "You, too, Bold. Just ask."

Bold nodded his thanks but said nothing. Sheila had taken a step that he had resisted for a long time now. Maybe it would be too late if he waited until he returned to Mongolia to further explore this Christian religion.

"Let's play a game," Sheila exhaled as she pushed out the suggestion, wanting to return them to the lighter mood of moments before.

"Sounds great," Ikota agreed and began clearing the table. Everyone joined in, and the dishes were done in a matter of minutes since they had cleaned up as they went along.

The games that followed made them think, brought on gales of laughter and strengthened their bonds of friendship. All tension was eased, and they all seemed to share a sense of release from the pressures they faced every day in this new country.

Bold had to drag himself away at 11:00 when Cheryl knocked on the door to take him home. That night he lay awake, thinking about the many things that had happened. He determined that he would ask Cheryl if he could host the group some Friday night. He finally drifted off to sleep, certain that she would be more than happy to help him.

Saturday morning Bold found himself in the kitchen with David. Everyone else was off running errands or doing chores. "How was your party last night, Bold?" David met his eyes and waited for a real answer, something he often did.

"It was fun. The food was good, and we played games and laughed a lot."

"You really have a great group of friends, Bold," David had a hint of jealousy in his voice but more happiness for Bold.

"Yes, I do. David, may I ask you about God? Do you really feel His Presence? Do you 'hear His voice' and 'see Him at work around you'?" Bold shifted uncomfortably in his chair, knowing that this conversation could change his life.

David seemed to also know this because he stopped eating his bowl of cereal and answered with carefully chosen words. "Yes, I hear God through the Bible, which I try to read every day. He inspired people to write what is in the Bible, so that those are His words to us. But I also hear Him during the quietness of prayer or when I'm in the midst of a dilemma that I can't handle by myself.

"During prayer I sometimes empty my mind of all the thoughts racing through it and wait for Him to answer a specific question or to let me know something that I've been missing. There are times when it is just peaceful and quiet, but other times He drops words into my mind that I know are from Him." Bold kept very still, not wanting to interrupt David's train of thought.

"I see Him in the beauty and magnificence of nature. I see Him in the love and kind acts of other Christians, especially my parents and little Cammy. I see Him in this house and this food," he indicated his cereal, "because I know it has been provided by God."

"But your dad works to provide these things," Bold insisted unable to let such a statement go by unchallenged.

"Yes, but He has provided my dad with the intelligence, the skills and the opportunity to earn the money to buy these things. I also know that even if something happened and my dad no longer had a job that my basic needs would be met because God has promised me that.

"It is hard to describe the sense of reality I have as I interact with God or my faith that He is always with me, but I never feel alone or abandoned. No matter what happens, I just know that God is there. I guess the fact that I have to believe He is there makes it more special and authentic to me." Bold could tell that David had begun to floundered with his words but also that David was deeply convinced of the things he shared with Bold. The self-assurance that was always mixed with concern for others reinforced David's words and convicted Bold's reticence to accept them as Truth.

"What does God demand from you if you believe in Him?" Bold searched for a loophole that would allow him a safe exit from this intense moment of decision.

"Nothing. The real work was done by Jesus who lived a perfect life, died for our sins and then rose from the dead, offering us the same perfection and future life with Him and God in Heaven. All He asks of us is that we believe."

"But you do not do what other teenagers do. You do not go to parties every weekend, and Christians are often teased at school. Others say they are 'too good', 'boring,' 'have no fun' and other things."

"You've been to our meetings, Bold. You know that we have fun. I've seen you laugh yourself," David lightly slapped Bold's forearm. "But we are also careful about how we live our lives, and we do care about what we do with our bodies. That's why parties where people get drunk, have to deal with hangovers the next morning and addictions the rest of their lives, don't really draw us. Sex is something else we value and want to save for the one special person we commit our lives to through marriage. These choices may make us appear to be boring, but they really are protecting us from future (and often immediate) regrets."

"Thank you, David, for being honest," Bold left without eating breakfast.

"You're welcome," David sent towards Bold's retreating back.

At dinner that evening Bold waited for a chance to join the lively banter but could not find a single break in the constant flow of words. So he forced an abrupt halt by saying, "I want to become a Christian."

"What?!" Cheryl's eyes filled with tears.

"Oh, goody, then you'll be my real brother," Cammy clapped in excitement.

"All right," David's eyes shone with a brightness and joy that made Bold's head swim. How could his decision affect others so powerfully?

"Would you like to pray right now, Bold, or would you like to come with me into the den to talk about it first?" Matt offered Bold some privacy.

"Now is okay. I am ready." Everyone bowed their heads, closing eyes shining with anticipation. "Dear God, thank you for bringing me to America and to this family. Thank you for dying that I can live. I believe in your Son Jesus and accept your salvation. Be as real to me as you are to the Bowers. Help me to be more real, too. Amen."

Tears flowed amidst laughter and hugs. Bold's cheeks glowed red with pleasure as he felt a chunk of ice of crash from his heart into the ocean of acceptance that flowed throughout his body, energizing him like nothing else had ever done before.

"I have so much to learn before I return home. Now I begin my real time in America." He told his newly discovered family.

"I'll help you," Cammy grabbed his hand and swung it in hers.

Bold finally felt released from all the anger and anxiety in which he had been suffocating.